THE CIRCLE BREAKERS

PATIENCE AGBABI

CANONGATE

First published in Great Britain in 2023 by Canongate Books Ltd,
14 High Street, Edinburgh EH1 1TE

canongate.co.uk

1

British Library Cataloguing-in-Publication Data
A catalogue record for this book is available on
request from the British Library

ISBN 978 1 83885 579 6

Typeset in Horley Old Style MT by
Palimpsest Book Production Ltd, Falkirk, Stirlingshire

Printed and bound in Great Britain by Clays Ltd, Elcograf S.p.A.

To the memory of my mum, Helen, for her mouth-watering
vegan feasts, quotes from the King James Bible
and passion for classical music.

Prose = words in their best order;
– Poetry = the *best* words in the best order.
                              – Samuel Taylor Coleridge

Unlike a great many painters who want to
be musicians, musicians who want to be
painters, and barristers who want to be
journalists, I want to be nothing in the
world except what I am – a musician.
                              – Samuel Coleridge-Taylor

Contents

Chapter 01:00

THE GHOST TRAIN

Halloween 2022 is fun but Halloween 2050 will be fantastic. There's a not-to-be-missed event at E-College-E, with a funfair and disco billed the best of the century. I've been conjuring it in my head to such fine detail I've barely slept all week. I don't do fancy dress so I'm wearing my favourite off-white retro tracksuit with a cotton skinsuit underneath so it doesn't itch at all. Under the right lights it will glow in the dark. 2050, here I come.

It's Monday the 31st of October 2022, 7.30 p.m., and The Infinites are in Room 4D at my school. It's a perfect cube; the walls, floor and ceiling the same pale cream. I'm a chameleon, blending in with the decor. We just finished youth club, run by Mrs C Eckler, where we watched a black-and-white film about time-travel made by a Leapling film-maker. When I first joined the school they used the room exclusively for leaping, but they changed the rules at the beginning of my Tenth Year to allow us to use it for extracurricular activities too. Room 4D is named after the fourth dimension, space–time. The first three dimensions are height, breadth and depth.

The Infinites are standing in a Chrono, a circle for leaping, in order of rank: MC^2, GMT, me, Big Ben and Portia. We're meeting Kwesi and Ama in 2050, the year they're based. Portia and Ama had their Infinite ceremonies last month so now we're seven strong.

'Does anyone have a spare leap band?' I say. 'I left— Oh, my phone!'

It's the deep buzztone that means another Chronophone is calling, not a regular mobile. I grab my silver Chronophone from my bag in time to see the name GRANDMA. She must be calling from work. I press the green button and her face fills the screen, all big-eyes and blue-green zigzag headtie.

'Elle, it is me, Grandma. Enjoy the party. Have a dance for me-o!'

I smile. Grandma has trouble walking, let alone dancing, but she still likes to have a go.

'Thank you, Grandma. Have you taken your tablets?'

She gives me a twisted smile which means no. Grandma has to take tablets for high blood pressure but she often 'forgets' to take them.

'Don't turn into a toad,' she says, which means be back by midnight.

'Grandma, I'll be back by 10.'

I mean it. Some days I don't like leaving Grandma alone for too long. She's become a bit confused about conversations she thinks we've had. I'm worried her memory's playing tricks on her.

'Greet that your friend, GT.'

Grandma has a soft spot for GMT because she's vegetarian, but always says her name wrong.

'I will, Grandma. She's here, right next to me. She can see and hear you!'

GMT leans over. 'Greetings, Mrs Ifíè.'

'Know thine enemy to defeat him. Godspeed!'

I say, 'Yes, Grandma!'

and GMT says, 'We sure will,'

at exactly the same time.

As soon as she's gone, MC² frowns at me.

'What's your gran on about? An' since when did she keep a Chronophone?'

'Nothing, really. Typical Grandma. She's always quoting stuff from the Bible about good conquering evil.' I pause. 'When I promised to get her a Chronophone so we could stay in touch when I'm on a mission, it turned out she's had one for years. She'd been hiding it in her room.'

'What colour?'

'Gold.'

He raises his eyebrows. 'Respect to Grandma. The gold came out in 2050; most reliable for a century. Your gran's a dark horse, Elle.'

Big Ben's frowning now. 'What's that mean?'

'Means,' says MC², 'she got talents she's keeping under wraps. Like us Leaps. Time to fast-forward.'

We hold hands. Big Ben is on my left; GMT on my right. I squeeze their hands and they squeeze mine back. We close our eyes, concentrate on the Fantastic Forest, E-College-E, the 31st of October 2050, 8 p.m. My fingers, toes, whole body fizz with energy as tiny white numbers begin to spin in the black vortex. I try to focus only on 2050 to stop myself feeling so nauseous. Grandma's call distracted me from borrowing a leap band to prevent it. Finally, the numbers slow down and stop.

I feel the mild, still air on my cheeks, smell pine and smoke, hear the rhythmic bass, howls and growls of beast beats in the background before I open my eyes. It's dark. The sky is dotted with what look like fluorescent giant bees but are actually people arriving via eco-jet. We're at the edge of the forest and ahead of us is a large field full of light and life, spiky marquees and bright white rides spinning so fast, they're almost invisible: the futuristic funfair. I can't wait!

∞

'Everything's powered by sun, wind or rain,' says Martin Aston aka Aston Martin, Big Ben's Annual friend who attends E-College-E and arranged tickets for us all. His wild straggly dark brown hair looks like it's been powered by sun, wind and rain too. I haven't seen him since our school trip to 2048 and he's grown 6 inches since. He's still not as tall as Big Ben, though, who's already managed to find the only meat stall in the whole field and has his mouth full of triple-decker burger. I don't have the heart to tell him it's not real meat. In the future, meat substitutes are so good you can't tell the difference. That's what our friend Season said and she's a super-taster cook, which means she has extra-sensitive tastebuds.

4

Talking of which, rumour has it Season's running a food stall here. Before leaving the house I made Grandma rice and fish stew which made my mouth water, but I wanted to save my appetite for Season's delicious vegan snacks. Her specialities are bread and coconut cake. She's autistic like me and Big Ben and loves cooking and eco-supercars.

'Fancy some food, sis?' says a familiar voice from behind me. 'Ama!'

She must have heard my stomach rumbling at the thought of food. My light-skinned, ginger afro'd friend comes into view, gives me a gap-toothed smile and the perfect bearhug. I find hugging difficult unless it's a firm squeeze. I smile back and bump fists with Kwesi standing next to her, a whole head taller but his ginger afro half the length of Ama's, his skin a tone darker. The family likeness is strong. It's great seeing all seven Infinites together. Of course, Aston Martin doesn't know we're a secret time-travelling crime-fighting group, but he DOES know all of us are Leaplings with The Gift of time-travel, except Ama, who's an Annual.

Then I notice a light-skinned black teen standing next to Kwesi, with an untidy afro, wearing a black hoodie and jeans that look too big to be making a fashion statement. If it weren't for his black hair, he could pass for Kwesi, a similar age (18), and build (athletic), but unlike Kwesi he looks at the ground all the time, avoiding our gaze. Ama sees me looking.

'Everyone. This is Samuel Coleridge-Taylor aka Coleridge, friend of Kwesi's from way back, staying at ours. Music maestro!'

Coleridge gives a small bow. I guess way back must mean another century rather than when they were young. Bowing is

5

retro. And he must have borrowed Kwesi's clothes. I realise I'm still staring at him because something's niggling me.

'Are you named after the poet Samuel Taylor Coleridge but the other way round?'

'I am,' replies Coleridge. 'I like poetry and music equally.'

He stares at the ground and I smile; we have something special in common.

Ama clears her throat theatrically. 'Are we going to stand here all night, or get something to eat?'

'Definitely food,' I reply. 'Have you seen Season's stall?'

'Follow me.' She begins walking into the crowds of teens wearing glow-in-the-dark bleeding heart or skeleton hoodies, pumpkin or monster helmets.

'Slow down, Leaps,' MC^2 calls after us. 'The Squared an' Kwesi wanna soundcheck with Coleridge for the Beat Battle later.'

'Portia and I got business to attend to,' says GMT.

Big Ben nods. 'Me and Aston Martin are going on Cars on Mars.'

'OK,' says Ama, 'how about we all meet in front of the Ghost Train at 9? The disco doesn't start till 9.30.'

∞

'What are you two doing here?' I say.

It's Jake and Maria, our friends from school. They're a couple now, though it's a bit on-off. Ama and I are queuing in front of Season's stall, which has a large sign outside saying SandWitches and Scream Cakes. There's such a big line, and Season's been so busy she hasn't seen us yet, but we can see her. She's still wearing

6

her black and silver hair in a knot on top of her head but she's added glitter for the occasion. Her nose piercing sparkles a midnight blue. The smell of smoky vegan food mixed with fresh bread is making my stomach rumble so much it sounds louder to me than the new background track of wind and waves.

'We're vegan now, you know,' says Maria, swishing back her head like she used to when she had long hair.

'Really?' I say, remembering Jake smuggling meat into a meat-free zone on our school trip to 2048.

'Since just now,' he grins, 'when we saw Season's stall.'

Suddenly, the teens ahead of us speed off like they're late for something; now we're at the front of the queue.

'Why, it's Elle!' says Season. 'And Ama and Jake and Maria. Where's . . . Big Ben?'

Sometimes it takes time for Season to find the right words. She calls it meaningful pausing and says it's her age but it might also be because she's autistic and takes a bit longer to process things. Lots of us have challenges with verbal language.

'He's at Cars on Mars with Aston Martin,' I say.

'Of course. Car-mad like me!' Season smiles. 'What would you like?' She lowers her voice. 'It's on the house for my favourite Leaplings.'

'A Full Moon SandWitch with your special white bread and a coconut cake for me,' I say.

'A Dark Moon SandWitch for me,' says Ama.

'Umm . . .' says Jake, 'you choose. It all looks great!'

'Two Vampire Bites and two Scream Cakes,' says Maria. 'Bet you'll love the cake, Jake.'

Season has everything ready in lightning speed like she leapt back in time a little to keep on top of the orders. As she hands us our food, she nods at the next people in the queue and smiles at us.

'Come and see me later if you get a chance.'

'OK,' we say, in unison.

As we walk off, I bite into my Full Moon SandWitch. The crust is crispy, the bread is light and airy, the cheese is creamy-crumbly. As delicious as I expected.

∞

The four of us are standing in front of Cars on Mars. There's a huge rust-red orb in the middle which must be Mars, and high in the sky multicoloured cars flying like satellites around it so slowly it's like they're floating in space. Then suddenly there's a hooting sound and they accelerate to breakneck speed, moving like they're weaving in and out of air traffic then diving over massive invisible speed bumps. Just watching them makes me feel dizzy and sick. But worst of all, there appears to be nothing connecting the cars to Mars; no chains or arms to be seen!

Jake and Maria have already joined the long queue, still devouring their Scream Cakes.

'You'll be sick,' I say from the sidelines.

'Who cares?' Jake takes the last mouthful of cake and begins to chew. 'You only live once.'

'The Carousel would be better,' says Maria. 'It has more style.'

8

'It wouldn't. The Carousel's retro: Cars on Mars is the future.' He pauses. 'Look who just got off!'

Big Ben and Aston Martin come into view. They're walking a bit funny and Big Ben's hair is even spikier than usual but their eyes are shining with excitement and they're talking to no one in particular, slightly too loud.

'Absolutely brilliant!' says Big Ben.

'Magnets,' says Aston Martin, slightly out of breath.

'Magnets from Mars.' Big Ben smiles at his wordplay.

So that's what connects the cars to the central orb. I watch as the two of them rejoin the queue and bump fists with Jake and Maria. Then Big Ben notices me and Ama.

'Come on Elle, it's like leaping.'

'No way! It would be hell for me.'

Occasionally, in his enthusiasm to include me, Big Ben forgets about my sensory sensitivities. I'm hypersensitive but he's hyposensitive, the exact opposite. He seeks out spicy food like pepper soup and loud sudden noises like fireworks, which make him feel great. He especially loves dangerous, thrilling rides – the faster the better.

'Don't forget the Ghost Train at 9,' I say.

'Elle,' says Ama, 'Maria's right. Fancy a ride on the Carousel?'

We walk through the crowds further across the field, in the opposite direction of the food stalls until we reach the retro rides area. I look at the gleaming silver-white merry-go-round slowing down in front of us and gasp. It's awesome, grotesque but magnificent at the same time. Two layers of red-flecked animals, with stairs between the floors, the smaller circle of creatures upstairs

9

hidden in darkness. The lower-deck creatures are larger than life: a horse with a blood-red saddle; a goat with jagged curly horns; a grimacing monkey that reminds me of someone but I can't think who; a ferocious cockerel with rubies for eyes; a dog baring its silver teeth; a pig that looks like it just swallowed a small child whole. They're so lifelike, the hairs stand up on the back of my neck.

I want to go on it; it would be fun and maybe as it's so retro it wouldn't go too fast and make me sick. But I still feel dizzy from watching Cars on Mars and on top of that, something else is stopping me. This circle of twisted animals reminds me of another circle, The Vicious Circle, Millennia's clock-inspired criminal gang.

'What's the verdict?' says Ama.

'Not now.' I pause. 'Can we do something with no spinning or bright lights? I'm a bit overloaded.'

'OK, sis. How about the Crystal Ball? We don't even have to queue.'

And without waiting for me to agree or disagree, Ama's striding towards the far end of the field until we find ourselves in a much more ambient space. You might think it's weird I'm checking out my future when I can leap to find out what it might be. But Ama made a good choice; it's just what I need at the moment, gentle lights and peace. The Crystal Ball is a large white dome tent with a massive mounted clear crystal in the middle that reminds me of a giant eyeball. All around the edge of the mount are seats, computer screens, controllers and what look like headphones. Ama drags me towards two free seats.

'Come on, sis! I want to see if I ever get to date MC^2.'

We both smile. Ama has liked MC^2 for years but now she's a fellow Infinite, she thinks it would spoil the group dynamic if they became a couple.

'How does it work?' I say, putting each pad onto my temples like Ama. They stick immediately and there's a gentle vibration that's quite pleasant but I have the strange feeling of someone listening to my innermost thoughts.

'Thought control, except the Ball's in charge, not you. They say it taps into your mind, like old-fashioned fortune tellers used to, and makes a prediction based on that. You get a printed card to take away. Since it's Halloween, most people get pumpkins, which they say means good luck but probably means you're having pumpkin pie for pudding.'

'So, if I think about running, it won't tell me what my PB will be next season?'

I've been trying to get my 100 metres time down to 12.52 seconds and have started training with the pentathletes to build up my strength. They do throwing and jumping as well as running.

'I doubt it will be accurate down to a hundredth of a second, Elle,' Ama grins to let me know she's joking – as if a machine could be THAT accurate – 'but it might tell you what you're running FROM. Ready?'

We both press the green START button on our controllers and I try to imagine it's the start of the 100-metre sprint, my hands behind the thick white line, my feet in the blocks. But instead, I find myself wondering whether Grandma has taken her tablets and, weirdly, remembering the grimacing monkey from the Carousel. I must be thinking hard because my mind begins to fizz like I'm leaping and I have to concentrate hard on the here and now to STOP myself from doing so. It would be disastrous for someone to see me disappear into thin air. Very few people know about The Gift. It has to remain top secret.

Then, just as quickly, the fizzy feeling goes and I breathe a sigh of relief. Ama already has her printout, a cartoon-style black cat, and she rolls her eyes anticlockwise. But nothing comes out of my machine. Maybe it's broken. Then I hear a strange whirring sound and a card flies out, followed by another. What can that mean? I pick them up off the floor. One's a grinning skeleton in a top hat; the other's a spider spinning a web. The pictures don't frighten me as they're silly cartoons, but TWO cards; I wasn't expecting that.

'It doesn't mean Death,' says Ama, misjudging my face. 'Skeleton means the end of one thing, start of another.'

'Why did I get two?' I frown as I zip the two cards safely into my tracksuit trouser pocket. I don't like the spooky feeling that the machine knows something I don't. I feel as if everyone knows what's happened and is staring at us, but none of the teens at the screens are paying us any attention. Ama shrugs.

'It probably malfunctioned. Maybe you were thinking about the Beat Battle. You can't trust technology, even in 2050. Come on, let's find the boys.' She drags me out of the tent before I can respond.

∞

The Ghost Train is the most atmospheric attraction of all. Its black front is embossed with glowing white ghosts, and the ride

12

itself is a glossy-black real miniature steam train with roofed, enclosed carriages. We arrive dead on 9 o'clock. Big Ben and Aston Martin are already standing in front of it eating BLACK candy floss. It looks like my hair when I comb it out into an afro.

'It'll rot your teeth,' I say but they ignore me.

'The Portal was brilliant!' Big Ben's mouth is full of sugar. 'You wear a thought-control helmet and make your own world.'

'We twinned up,' says Aston Martin. 'Never seen so many Lambos in my life.'

'So you didn't spend the whole time on Cars on Mars.' I smile.

Big Ben nods. 'Last queue was 30 minutes long. The Portal had no queue so we went there instead.'

'Glad you had fun,' says Ama. 'Crystal Ball botched.'

'Hey guys.' It's GMT, slightly breathless. 'Portia's busy as a bee, she'll meet us in the discotheque. Seen any ghosts yet?'

'No such thing,' says Big Ben between bites.

'Just cos you never saw one.' GMT frowns. 'Ghosts don't have to be dead folks; living folks can haunt you too.'

'Zombies,' says Aston Martin, doing monster-eyes. 'The living dead.'

'Watch out,' says GMT. 'We Leaplings often come back after we're dead and buried!'

'How's that, then?'

'If we leaped into the future when we were alive, beyond the date we died.'

Aston Martin raises his eyebrows. I don't blame him. If you don't hang out with Leaplings often, you forget what we can do.

There's a rush of air, three outlines in the dark, then Kwesi,

13

MC^2 and Coleridge appear close beside us. GMT jumps and looks cross.

'Too lazy to trek across a field. Want the world to see you leap?'

'The trio was running late.' MC^2 shrugs.

We look across at the Ghost Train. It doesn't look like there are any other passengers for the ride. A short teen dressed as Dracula complete with death-white face, fangs, long dark cloak and black gloves stands on the platform.

'Leaving in one minute,' he says. 'Best ride outside London.'

Maybe it's the fangs distorting his voice that make me shudder. And something about his face reminds me of the monkey from earlier. He's putting me off riding the Ghost Train.

'Doesn't the disco start soon?' I say.

'In half an hour,' says MC^2. 'We got stacks of time. Come on, Leaps!'

'You all go, I'll wait here.'

I can feel the two cards in my tracksuit pocket. What do they mean? Maybe that's why I suddenly feel so anxious. The cards, the Carousel, Cars on Mars. It's all too much for my system. I need some quiet time alone.

'Scared?' says Aston Martin.

Big Ben shakes his head. 'Elle's not scared. She's brave!'

Big Ben always sticks up for me, I love that about him. But I AM scared, scared I'll go into shutdown and miss the Beat Battle and the disco. I'm extra sensitive and often pick up on things other people don't. No one else seems bothered. Big Ben continues.

14

'Elle, we should stay together. Safer on the Ghost Train than out here alone.'

'30 seconds,' says Dracula.

I make up my mind. I feel almost sick with fear but The Infinites should definitely stick together, look out for each other like we always do. I take a very deep breath and nod as we get into the ride. I sit down in a carriage with Big Ben beside me, Aston Martin and Ama opposite; MC², Kwesi, Coleridge and GMT are in the carriage behind us. The seats are comfy, luxurious red velvet, not what I expected at all. I thought they'd be black and peeling, with fake rats or something coming out of them. We hear a shrill whistle, the train judders forwards – we're off!

I've been on ghost trains before. Usually, the carriages are open so I feel cobwebs on my face and hear screams and see skeletons and witches trying to grab at me. They're not scary because they're all the same. But this is totally different. It's scary because I DON'T see, feel or hear those things. This is a real train and, for some reason, I sense real danger. My heart is pumping hard in my chest. I'm only afraid of the unknown, and this is a trip into the unknown.

I hold Big Ben's hand tight, like we're leaping. I close my eyes and take deep breaths to calm myself down. None of it works. My body begins to go fizzy and I freeze, scared for the second time tonight that I'm going to leap by mistake. And now behind my eyelids I see the numbers; dates going back in time, fuzzy white on black. Big Ben squeezes my hand even tighter. I open my mouth to tell Ama and Aston Martin what's happening but no sound comes out. No one says anything but I hear one of them take a sharp breath in; I open my eyes in time to see their eyes widen in horror. They know what's happening, too, even though they're Annuals.

We're leaping back in time.

This is no ordinary ghost train. This is a trap and there's nothing we can do but sit here and wait for it to stop.

It stops.

I open my eyes.

It's still dark outside.

'Leaps,' shouts MC^2 from the carriage behind us. 'Out! Now!'

We fumble for the doors and spill out into the night. We're on the edge of the forest like before but there's no funfair in the field ahead. Just the cold night air. I look around at my friends to see that even Kwesi, the calmest of us all, looks shaken. We instinctively huddle together, waiting to see what happens next.

What happens turns my heart to ice.

'Welcome to 1880,' says the driver of the Ghost Train.

Fear and anger rise up in me. I should have trusted my instincts; I shouldn't have listened to Big Ben. Because now I know who the monkey reminded me of.

The Ghost Train driver has removed his fangs and put on a tall top hat but he looks more sinister than ever. His deathly white skin glows in the dark; he looks at us with his slate-grey eyes. Oh my Chrono! It can't be; it is. The evil teen, the malevolent Ancient, Millennia's right-hand man, number Eleven of The Vicious Circle: The Grandfather.

Chapter 02:00

THE GRANDFATHER'S PARADOX

'My favourite year, 1880. And today's my favourite day,' says The Grandfather. 'Guess the date!'

'We don't have to,' I say. 'We have Chronophones.'

That was my voice speaking before I had time to stop it. Why should we engage with The Grandfather when he's just kidnapped all eight of us? We're bunched up and holding hands, ready to leap if we have to.

'Think you'll find,' he smiles his vicious smile, 'your Chronophones won't work proper. Not yet. Took you the scenic route.'

'What does that mean?'

'Via the Liverpool and Manchester Railway, 1830, first major train route in Britain. Welcome to the Age of the Railway.'

MC^2 body blinks so fast, he's a blur. 'What do you want?'

The Grandfather steps back. I think he's scared of MC^2. That sounds like one of MC^2's rhymes. I wish we were at the Battle of the Beats and not here. But then I realise he's not scared, he's stepping back for dramatic effect.

'Don't know what happened in the leap year 1880? Leaplings, you surprise me.'

We DO know but we're not going to tell him. Every Leapling learns about the Statutes (Definition of Time) Act in Tenth Year of school. On the 2nd of August 1880, Britain legally adopted Railway Time, which is Greenwich Mean Time, as the national standard. Before then, all the cities in the UK had different times like different countries do now. Except they weren't hours different, just minutes. But minutes could make a big difference if you wanted to avoid a train crash! It must be the 2nd of August. I wonder why he's chosen this date.

'We ain't here to play school,' says MC². 'Get to the point or—'

'Somethin' to spark you. Somethin' to get your teeth into.'

I'm reminded of the fangs he was wearing as Dracula, the way they distorted his voice. But now his voice is clear and confident, not the voice of a boy-man but the voice of a man-boy. The Grandfather revels in his meaningful pause. He theatrically fumbles in his cloak for several seconds before pulling out a bat-black envelope with a blood-red seal like something from the Museum of the Past, the Present and the Future.

'An anonymous note was delivered to my door today. Might be in your interest to read it.'

I narrow my eyes at him. 'What does it say?'

He holds out his black-gloved hand. 'Take it, Elle, and find out for yourself. You don't need to take it to the committee.' He eyes everyone behind me with malevolence. 'Two can solve it. You an' Big Ben.'

'Why us?' I say. 'Why not The Vicious Circle?'

'Because,' he says, staring me straight in the eye till it's like a drill in my head and I look away, 'you think different. You see details others don't. You work stuff out.'

He knows about us finding the Infinity-Glass and probably the case of the missing Leaplings too. I can't deny it: Big Ben and I are good at solving mysteries because we're autistic. Big Ben's very logical and I remember things like playing back a film in my head. But how could we possibly work for our enemy?

'Tell Millennia we won't do it!'

'Ha!' I wince at The Grandfather's monosyllabic laugh. 'Millennia? She don't know nothing about this. The note was delivered to me, my private business. Anyway,' he continues, 'wouldn't trust her far as I could throw her. I help old ladies cross the timeline not run the show.'

I raise my eyebrows. I know The Vicious Circle hate each other but I thought Millennia and The Grandfather were loyal. And it doesn't make sense. Millennia's number Twelve and The Grandfather's number Eleven so surely SHE's in charge. It's like he reads my mind.

'Who founded The Vicious Circle? The Grandfather. Who made her Twelve only cos she lives in the 21st century and got connections? The Grandfather. Who wants me dead and buried 10 feet deep? Millennia. And there's the paradox all Leaplings know from the year dot: The Grandfather Paradox. She can't kill ME. If she kills me, her grandfather, she won't never be

19

born and if she's never born she can't kill me. Ha! I'd kill her for getting too big for her boots but it'd be like killing me own grandmother. Besides, I'm having too much fun.'

'Even if she could, why would she kill you if you're dead already?' I say. 'You died in 1925!'

He winces but only for a split second. 'So what if I did? I'm alive now, 14. Same age as you. Plenty of seconds to ride the timeline.'

'How do you know how old I am?'

'Easy to work out Leapling ages. Elle, I know more about you than you do. I live in three centuries. In this one, already running me own clockshop, Moon & Sons. Take a visit and meet my older self. He thinks he's better than me cos he speaks proper but I always have the last word. Oh, I forgot. Two of you already met him.' He looks at GMT and MC^2, who look away, embarrassed. GMT stole watches from The Grandfather's shop in the past and MC^2 sold them in the future. 'Don't worry, he's harmless. Pretending to be an Annual and cares more about clocks than fisticuffs. I help him run the family business. I loathe him.'

I can't help but smile at The Grandfather disliking his future self in the past.

'Maybe you grow up better,' I say.

'I do but it don't become me.' He stares into my eyes. 'Take the letter and cut the small talk. Doesn't become YOU.'

He holds out his hand again, stares at me and drops the black envelope onto the grass. Big Ben immediately leaps forward and picks it up. I do big-eyes. What if it has poison on it? The Grandfather was wearing gloves.

20

Now he nods at Big Ben. 'Clever boy. You might find it hard to read but you'll understand the urgency.'

I'm shocked he knows Big Ben is dyslexic. How does he know so much about us? The Grandfather pulls himself up till he's 2 inches taller.

'Find out who wrote it and report back to me.'

The Infinites only report to Infinity, the wisest bissextile of all who no one's ever seen. But I don't say this out loud. It's top secret.

'What place, date and time was it delivered?' says Big Ben.

'Good question. It came to my clockshop today at noon. Might be significant, all the clocks of the UK getting in synch.'

'Who delivered it?'

'Usual postboy in the usual carriage. No stamp cos it was sent private. Nothing unusual there.'

'How do we contact you?'

'Dial 1852, my birth year. But I need a number for you.'

Big Ben says, 'My number's 0666,' before I can stop him and The Grandfather taps it into his Chronophone.

'Glad you have the sense to cooperate.'

'Do we get a reward?' says Big Ben.

I'm shocked that Big Ben wants to take on a job from The Grandfather AND is asking for money. Maybe it's because we got £10,000 for solving the last crime. Then I realise he's not thinking money for himself; he's thinking about me and Grandma, how we used some of that money to do up our flat. Money doesn't motivate Big Ben, he just loves problem-solving, but he's kind and always looks out for his friends.

The Grandfather narrows his eyes at Big Ben.

'You're too good for your own good. You don't want money; you want to save the world. That'll be your reward.' He pauses and stares at me with his cold grey eyes. 'As for you, do it for your grandma. Make her proud!'

I narrow my eyes at him. 'Leave Grandma out of this.'

He shakes his head. 'You got so much to learn, Elle. But it ain't my job to teach you. Time will tell. And now, if you'll permit me, I'll take my leave. Business to attend to.'

The Grandfather doffs his hat and disappears into thin air, leaving the eight of us standing in the night field, our mouths a capital O. Big Ben puts the envelope carefully into his rucksack but I look at it like it's a bomb about to go off.

What does the letter say and why did The Grandfather ask Big Ben and me to decipher it? And what was all that stuff about Grandma? I have a feeling in my bones there's something suspicious about the whole thing. I want to ignore it but I can't. He kidnapped us via the Ghost Train to give us the letter. It must be super important. Everything hinges on what's inside. But I don't want to open it. I won't open it. Not yet.

Chapter 03:00

SONOS AND CHRONOS

The Battle of the Beats is taking place in the E-College-E school hall, which has been decorated with glowing pumpkins and fake cobwebs. All The Infinites plus Coleridge are here. I look around for Jake and Maria but they must have gone home. And, thankfully, no sign of The Grandfather. I hope he stayed in 1880 and won't spoil the rest of our evening. I can't wait to see Kwesi and MC^2 compete. We're standing in the shadows near the back of the room.

The Battle of the Beats is in full flow. We've had almost an hour of spoken word over what often sounds like a heartbeat. Each duo performs their piece with backing music then a panel of three judges marks them, holding up score cards for marks out of 10 and the crowd boo or cheer depending on whether each judge has been accurate or harsh. The judges are older than the audience, two women and one man, probably teachers, but I don't recognise any of them. Ambient music is played in between each act while the judges do their marking, like now.

This track is called 'Raindance' and the crowd whip themselves up into a frenzy. Some teens have their hands in the air, palms facing upwards as if commanding the sky to break open. Others are rapidly stamping on the spot. The air is suffused with tiny dots like real drizzle and some teens press their temples until bright yellow umbrellas seem to sprout from their heads. Then the bass kicks in, the rumble of thunder, and mock forked lightning zigzags the room. Everyone jerks and some of the teens end up on the floor, playing dead. After two minutes, the music fades, the crowd grumble and the three judges hold up cards for the previous duo: 5, 6 and 5. The crowd don't disagree: it wasn't very good.

'Thank you, judges,' says the host, Mrs Storm, the teacher with purple hair we met on our 2048 trip. 'And next on stage, we have "Bat Battle", with sounds by Sonos, choreography by Chronos and rhymes by Destiny. Give them an E-College-E welcome!'

There's a slow trickle of applause, like light rain spitting from the previous track. The crowd are still cross their favourite tune was cut short. But it slowly builds into more polite clapping and as it does, I'm aware of two things: Portia standing beside me picks her bag up off the floor at the same time that I notice a whirring noise, movement above my head and large shadows projecting all over the walls, making me feel nauseous even though I try not to look.

But I can't help but look up to the ceiling like everyone else because swooping around the room are two giant bats with black webbed wings, yellow pointed teeth and protruding eyes, arriving by eco-jet. When I say giant, I mean teenager size, which is exactly what they are. What a fantastic disguise! The two bats land on the stage on either side of the host, who looks a bit shaken.

'Well,' she says, 'that was a dramatic entrance. Which of you is Sonos and which is Chronos?'

'I'm Sonos,' says the slightly taller bat on her left in a rich deep voice.

'And I'm Chronos,' says the bat on her right a split second later, like he's finishing off the sentence.

'Could you tell us something about your piece?'

Sonos clears his throat. 'We like bats because bats get a bad press they don't deserve. It fitted with Halloween and the eco scene. So Destiny wrote us rhymes.'

'We thought it was time,' continues Chronos, 'to set the record straight.'

I smile at the wordplay and then I frown. Chronos means time, like Chrono. With a name like that, surely he must be a Leapling? The moment I think it, I'm aware of a slight gust of air beside me. Portia was right next to me a moment ago. Now she's gone. I look around. I'm not sure the others noticed. MC² and Kwesi might have known what Portia's up to but they're behind the scenes, getting ready to go on stage.

Why did Portia leave? She LOVES music, she wouldn't miss this for the world. What on earth's going on? But I don't have time to work it out because, over a backbeat of high-pitched shrieking that makes me put my hands over my ears, Sonos and Chronos begin their double act.

'Call me Sonos . . .'

'Call me Chronos . . .'

'Master of tempo . . .'

'Master of tempus . . .'

Although I HATE the backbeat, Sonos and Chronos are good. They perform so seamlessly it's like one person rapping rather than two, but their voices make a great contrast like they really are bats battling each other and the rhymes are sharp. Whilst they're performing, a petite white girl with untidy, mousy hair dressed head to toe in black, complete with webbed wings, inches towards the stage. She's nodding her head to the beat, mouthing the words as they say them.

She must be Destiny. I wonder why she didn't want to perform on stage since she wrote the lyrics. Maybe she likes to control everything behind the scenes but doesn't like being in the lime-light herself. But almost all the performers have been duos, so nothing unusual there. She certainly can't be shy, dressing up like a bat.

I can tell their piece is about to finish because the whirring noise begins again, the eco-jets ready to take off. And that's exactly what they do; first Sonos, then Chronos. Off they go, up they go, into the wings. The crowd show their appreciation, the ambient music comes on, this time bug beat, and Destiny turns away from the stage. I try to look away but I can't help noticing her eyes: bulbous and piercing, like a bat's.

A minute later the music fades and the judges hold up their cards: 9, 8 and 10, a total of 27 out of 30! The crowd come back to life with cheers and whoops and Destiny smiles. The marks were fair: if it wasn't for the backing track, they might have got full marks. But not everyone has my taste in music; maybe they lost a few marks because of the lyrics or the bat costumes. We'll never know. But I do know this: MC^2 and Kwesi have to do the performance of a lifetime to beat them.

The host takes to the stage once more, her purple hair highlighted by the spotlights.

'Very well done, Sonos and Chronos, the first 10 of the night.' She pauses. 'And last but not by any means least, we have "Ghosts" with words by MC^2, sign-dance by Kwesi and musical arrangement by The Maestro. E-College-E and friends, put your hands together!'

MC^2 and Kwesi appear from the back of the stage whilst Coleridge, aka The Maestro, walks through the audience to the back of the room, where he stands alone. I'm pleased. I was worried they'd try to outdo the previous act with a grand entrance, like disappearing and reappearing on the spot in true MC^2 fashion, which would blow our Leapling cover. But I'm still wondering what they're going to do. They've been keeping their piece a secret. As they reach the stage, someone shouts 'Nuclear!' and MC^2 waves.

The host smiles warmly. 'MC^2 and Kwesi are well known for their double act, but we would love to hear what has inspired this latest piece.'

'It's a new take on Halloween. Ghosts are the species destroyed by industrialisation and global warming,' says MC^2, blinking, and Kwesi signs as he speaks. 'All the creatures we no longer see in the sea or the air or the bush or the field or the tree . . .'

It's like Kwesi has suddenly become a creature himself. He signs with his whole body in the exact rhythm of MC²'s lyrics. It's Standard Sign Language, the international sign language of the future, with his own flamboyant finger-snaps and facial expressions. And softly, so quietly you almost can't hear it, the chirping of crickets begins as a backbeat.

> 'Thrum on the drum for the humming-bird,
> heart skip a beat for the bumblebee,
> humble myself to the drumbeat . . .'

As the list gets longer, the backbeat becomes a chorus of lost animals and Kwesi inhabits each line, each insect, mammal, fish and fowl. I feel as if I'm INSIDE their piece, like the Amazonian rainforest before it was cut down. I feel totally connected to nature and also grief for all the creatures that are no longer with us. I look around the audience. They're feeling it too, swaying to the beat but not like they were before. They're listening, savouring every single word. And at the back of the hall, Coleridge is animated, conducting the piece with his fingertips.

At the very end of the piece, Kwesi does a sign-solo in his own unique sign language that's much faster and more energetic than Standard Sign Language. It's as if he's actually become every insect, bird, mammal and fish from the rap, in quick succession. Between each one, for a nanosecond, he disappears. Only a Leapling could spot it; everyone else sees a trick of the light. The message is clear: all these creatures are Ghosts.

When he's finished, there's silence for a split second before the crowd erupt into manic applause. Some teens have tears streaming down their faces. MC² and Kwesi leave the stage and come back to stand with us but the audience are still applauding. Everyone loved it. Big Ben gives them a huge grin.

'You were best,' he says.

Gentle background music fades in as the judges make their decisions. No one dances this time. The atmosphere has changed completely. It was sad but appreciative; now it's tense. How will the judges respond? They flip over their scores: 10, 10, 6! A total of 26. I can't believe it. The booing begins, increasing in volume like a dinosaur waking up after a long sleep. I put my hands over my ears but it doesn't go away. It's a very specific displeasure directed at the third judge, an older man with a mop of white hair wearing a silver tunic who looks like a futuristic version of Einstein. He obviously didn't like or didn't GET the lyrics.

The purple-haired host takes to the stage looking even more shaken than when Sonos and Chronos arrived as bats.

'Silence, please!' she says. 'It is fine to show your displeasure but the judges' decision is final. The winners of the 2050 E-College-E Battle of the Beats are Sonos and Chronos and Destiny. Please give them a round of applause for their fantastic piece as they take to the stage to collect their prize.'

About half the crowd applaud as this time the trio walk to the stage in their bat costumes. But I'm not looking at them. I'm narrowing my eyes at the third judge with the wild Einstein hair who gave my friends 6 out of 10. He's looking up at the stage and I see a look pass between him and Destiny. It's only for a split second but it happens. Then I know. He wasn't an impartial judge at all. He must know Destiny and that's why he gave MC², Kwesi and The Maestro such a low mark. So that she and her crew could win. I HATE unfairness. No one else has noticed but I hope one day it will come back to haunt him. As Grandma says, cheats don't prosper.

Then I look back at Sonos and Chronos up on stage receiving their prize and my eyes widen. They've both taken off their bat goggles so their black skin and eyes are visible and I recognise them for who they really are. I've seen them once before when I myself was in disguise and infiltrated a criminal meeting by accident and I never forget a face: the master of tempo and the master of tempus are Two and Three of The Vicious Circle! And that makes me wonder, who is Destiny?

Chapter 04:00

THE KEY NOTE

When it all gets too much for me in the future, I go underground. Underground is going to Ama and Kwesi's subterranean house, which always makes me feel calm. Ama's dad's an architect and her mum's an eco-nomist so they designed their own home. From the 2030s more and more people commissioned their own eco-homes and rather than build up, they built down. The houses are called eartheaters, the polar opposite of skyscrapers.

How can I go straight home after everything that just happened? I need time to process the night's events, so all The Infinites plus Coleridge but minus Portia have come back to Ama's. Her parents are out at a Halloween party so they won't be back till after midnight. It's just gone 11 o'clock when we arrive outside the wooden front door which is built into a mound. At exactly the same time, we hear a low engine purr and see headlights descending onto Ama's drive and a flash of silver. I squint; Portia's Porsche. She traded in the Leaping Lamborghini for a smaller car and cash. She says this has better handling but I prefer the wordplay. She gets out and marches across the gravel.

'Sorry I disappeared earlier. Gutted I missed the Battle. Stuff's happening.'

We nod, knowing that Portia will update us soon. She's good like that; the best double agent ever, an Infinite who works for The Vicious Circle but they don't suspect. But at the moment I can't take anything else in; I just need to get inside the house. Before Ama has a chance to get out her mobile to activate the door, it flies open and Robot, Ama's freshly created companion, appears. Robot looks like a metallic scarecrow that isn't scary; a human-like figure dressed in shabby old clothes. Ama wants to work in robot design so took the Artificial Intelligence option at school and collaborated to create a companion who happily does the jobs she dislikes.

'How was the Halloween? Would you like some snacks?'

Ama smiles. 'It was great. Yes, lemonade and snacks would be great. We'll be in the games room this time, not the pool.'

Big Ben frowns. 'Is Robot like a servant?'

He hasn't met Robot at Ama's house before.

'Yeah!' says Ama. 'Programmed to do the housework and homework. And to have lots of fun on their days off!'

'Brilliant!' says Big Ben.

I know what he's thinking: maybe Robot can help him write essays. Maybe they could. I notice Coleridge staring at Robot disappearing into the kitchen, eyes Jupiter-large. Although he's Kwesi's friend and is staying with them, he must find all the futuristic stuff a bit of a culture shock.

We descend to the lower ground floor on the eco-lator, which is an escalator made of wood and run by wind. The games room is massive enough for me to decompress whilst the others talk. One wall has a shelf on it with every board game imaginable; another wall is taken up by a giant screen for computer games. In the corner is my favourite silver running machine and that's what I go on now. I just need to get into the zone for ten minutes and I'll be better able to work through each of tonight's events. At the moment, they're tangled up in my head like a spaghetti junction: I want them to look like a motorway stretching into the far distance, each event a straight line. I know they're interconnected but I have to see them as separate issues first.

As I get into the zone, the main events of the evening enter my mind in order: the Crystal Ball; the Ghost Train; and the Beat Battle. I begin to relax and the occasional word from the others' conversation filters through, like 'bats', 'they'd recognise me' and 'whole thing fixed'. I'm aware Robot has served snacks and the focus shifts to food. I'm surprised to hear Coleridge's quiet voice amidst the general chat.

'Are these bananas of the future?'

'Plantain chips,' says Ama. 'Plantain's a cooking banana popular in West Africa. You should go to Elle's in 2022 and eat them fresh. They only import dried stuff now.' She pauses. 'Get Elle to cook you jellof rice too; she's an amazing cook.'

'I would much appreciate that,' says Coleridge, 'since I wish to taste more of my culture.' He doesn't sound like a teen at all. He sounds like a grown-up.

'I'm coming too!' says Big Ben.

'Of course, BB,' I say, slowing down on the treadmill. 'If Coleridge can make this Thursday, we can cook for him together.'

Big Ben comes to tea after school most Thursdays after we've done our homework in Room 4D. Big Ben enjoys helping me cook and LOVES Nigerian food; he doesn't even cough after the hottest pepper soup.

I speed up again and before long, I cut out all background noise. I'm back in the zone. Even though I'm on the treadmill, I'm somewhere else, literally, in my head. When I get into the zone, everything from outside disappears, my senses no longer on high alert all the time. I'm able to just be in my body. I'm aware of my blood pumping, my muscles working hard, my limbs in perfect synchronisation, my temperature rising and the sweat darkening the armpits of my skinsuit. I'm at peace. My thoughts slow down and separate and I begin to see things clearly. I have my best insights when I'm running.

That happens now. I replay the scene in my head when Sonos and Chronos took to the stage and that knowing look passed between the evil judge and the tiny rhymer. A word crystallises in my head: Destiny.

I gradually slow down on the treadmill. If you stop too abruptly on running machines, you get thrown across the room. Even though I want to talk immediately, I have to let my body catch up with my mind.

'Who's Destiny?' I say.

Everyone looks at me then looks away, apart from Big Ben who's closed his eyes as he does when he's solving a maths problem. The others are sprawled on bean bags the other side of the room, munching plantain and yam chips and drinking the homemade lemonade that I always thought Ama's dad made but I now wonder if it's made by Robot. Ama's programmed the windows to show the night sky with a full moon gleaming through one of them, its rays shining on me. I feel like I'm in the spotlight.

Portia jumps slightly at the name Destiny. 'Funny you should ask; I'm wondering that myself. You know my uncle Nano finally went to prison last week for his illegal landfill? And Sonos and Chronos are in The Vicious Circle? Well, today Millennia promoted us. I'm now Two, Sonos is Three and Chronos took Uncle's place as Four. I didn't tell you earlier, you were all so focused on the night out.' She pauses to sip her lemonade. 'That meant there was a vacancy for One. Destiny just joined The Vicious Circle! The other Elders are furious, as they weren't consulted, but Millennia's word is final.'

The Elders of The Vicious Circle are numbers Ten to Twelve: Meridian, The Grandfather and Millennia. Meridian disagrees with everything Millennia says and The Grandfather admitted to us this evening that he doesn't trust Millennia. They all hate each other. No wonder they're not happy about Destiny; if Millennia had asked them, they would have voted against getting a new member they didn't know.

'Why d'ya ask about Destiny, Elle?' says MC^2.

'Destiny knows the judge who marked you and Kwesi down. I could tell by the way they looked at each other. And she obviously hangs out with Sonos and Chronos. I mean Three and Four.'

Portia frowns. 'Fill me in. What happened? I had to leap away when they announced their act. If any of them saw me with you lot, I'd be exited on the spot.'

She means kicked out of The Vicious Circle but the word exited sounds more sinister than that. They've already made Portia work for The Vicious Circle for life; what would they do to her if they found out she was a member of The Infinites and working with us, their arch enemies?

We update Portia on everything that happened at the Beat Battle this evening and she nods, pursing her lips.

'That judge was probably Otto, number Eight on The Vicious Circle. He fits the description. Interesting he knows Destiny already.'

Big Ben opens his eyes like he just woke up. '*DESTINY*'s a gameshow. My mum watches it. She gets tickets to be in the audience but never goes. There's a circle with 12 symbols around it and it spins until one of them lights up.'

Big Ben's describing the start of the show. He must mean the 12 signs of the Zodiac.

'What you sayin', bro?' says MC[2] but Kwesi answers, signing rapidly, and MC[2] translates for us all. 'Kwesi says Destiny got her own show in real time, 2022, where she interviews minor celebrities and predicts what they want to know about the future. When they'll get married, that kind of spit.' He rolls his eyes and Ama looks sad for a split second but only I see it. 'But some folks want to know serious stuff.'

'Like what?' I ask.

'Like whether there'll be World War Three, how long the planet will last . . .'

I frown. 'Is Destiny a Leapling? If she is, she could leap forward in time and find stuff out then report back to the programme.'

'Yes,' says Big Ben, 'but only what MIGHT happen.'

'OK,' I say. 'We're in the future now. Is this only what COULD happen rather than what definitely WILL happen?'

'Correct. We're in one of an infinite possibility of futures.' Big Ben smiles at his wordplay.

'Well,' says Ama, 'I'm very happy living in this possible version of 2050, apart from little miss Destiny and Otto messing with the Beat Battle score. MC^2 and Kwesi won tonight. Can't we go back and change it?'

'We COULD,' says Big Ben, 'because the future isn't fixed. But it's hard to change only one thing. You end up changing other things and it gets complicated.'

'Guys,' says GMT, 'I love chatting about time-travel conundrums as much as you but we're forgetting something.' She pauses. 'The Ghost Train. 1880. The Grandfather.'

Portia goes pale. 'You met The Grandfather? You're obsessing about the Beat Battle but not—'

'Not obsessing. It was me,' I say. 'I wanted to know about Destiny. We were going to tell you about the Ghost Train. So much happened tonight.'

As GMT explains to Portia, who shudders whenever Ama fills in more details, Big Ben hunts in his bag and reveals the bat-black envelope with the blood-red seal. Here, in Ama's massive futuristic games room, it looks like we've committed an Anachronism, a crime across time, by stealing an object from an earlier era. The envelope looks totally out of place in 2050.

'Shall I open it?' asks Big Ben.

We all look at each other, our minds wandering back to that damp field in 1880, The Grandfather's challenge to me and Big Ben. I know what we have to do but my instinct says no, it's too dangerous. Portia looks very serious when she speaks.

'If we open it, we must open it now, when we're all together and can help each other. I know The Grandfather said Elle and Big Ben should go it alone but I disagree. I know him, I know his methods and I don't trust him an inch.'

'That's exactly what he said about Millennia,' I say.

Kwesi signs opening a letter and draws the infinity symbol in the air, reminding us who we are and what we stand for: a youth group that fights crime on the timeline for a better, greener future. We mustn't be cowards; we must stand up to our enemies.

'BB,' I say, 'let's open it together.'

Whilst Big Ben holds the envelope, I carefully prise it open. The note inside the envelope is white but the writing isn't handwriting, it's a combination of letters cut out of a newspaper. This is what is says:

Make me Midnight,
Chrono of Crime,
or I'll tell the world
we can leap through time.

I read it out loud for the benefit of Big Ben before placing the note on a table for everyone to see. Coleridge seems particularly interested in it, frowning and tapping his fingers.

'Whoever composed the note is partial to the music of words,' he says. 'It reminds me of the Beat Battle this evening.'

'I thought that too,' I reply. 'I love the alliteration in the first line and the punchiness of it.'

He smiles as if to encourage me to say more but I hold it in. Sometimes I pay too much attention to sound and not enough to sense, especially when I'm listening to music from the 1960s. In this case, the message is too important for that to happen. And we have to explain the context of the message to Coleridge; he isn't an Infinite. He doesn't know about our enemies and wouldn't have understood our earlier chat about Destiny's promotion.

'It's a message for The Vicious Circle, an evil gang,' I say. 'They call themselves Chrono of Crime when they have their meetings. Twelve of them sit at a circle like a clockface and they each have a number.'

'In music they would be a Circle of Fifths and use letters for the scales,' says Coleridge. 'It connects the 12 tones in Western music. But the outside letters are different to those on the inside.'

Portia nods. 'Yes. The Vicious Circle is definitely like that. Not everyone's what they seem on the outside. I'm Two but a double agent.'

Big Ben has his eyes closed. 'Midnight is 12 o'clock so it must be Millennia.'

'Millennia's the leader of The Vicious Circle,' I add. 'The note says, "Make me Midnight". Whoever wrote it wants to be the leader instead. They want to get rid of Millennia.'

'Or they'll spill the beans on Leaps with The Gift,' says MC². 'It's serious spit! The Squared says we gotta act quick. Ain't just The Vicious Circle under threat; it's all of us.' He pauses to let his words sink in and it's like we've all stopped breathing. 'The Oath has kept us secret for centuries. Some Annuals guessed but kept quiet. I broke the rules myself but only when I knew it was safe. Who made this note?'

At that precise moment, Robot enters the room and collects the used cups and plates onto an elbow-level inbuilt tray that appears at the press of a button. Big Ben narrows his eyes at Robot and points at the collaged sheet on the table.

'Robot, who made the note?'

'*The Times*, Monday, August 2, 1880,' says Robot.

I smile as Robot leaves the games room. Robot didn't answer the question the way we wanted but has given us a bit of a clue. The note was made from a newspaper of the same day it was delivered, the day that time was standardised in Britain. It might be relevant. But we hardly have any more clues. I frown and think aloud.

'It could have been made by anybody.'

Big Ben's shaking his head. 'Not ANYBODY. Everyone except Millennia; she's already the leader. And someone who likes typefaces. Not me!'

'True,' I say, 'unless Millennia wrote the note to get at The Grandfather in some way. But BB, they used a newspaper collage to hide their identity, not because they liked the look of them.'

'Good work,' says MC². 'Don't take nothin' at face value. Anyone could be a suspect.'

'Guys,' says GMT, 'I suggest Elle and Big Ben brainbuzz together and report back to the group when they've made some progress. It's been a long day and we all need to chill.'

Big Ben hands the note to me; he obviously wants me to be in charge of it. I put it back into the envelope and push it deep into my bag. GMT's right about needing to chill; I'm exhausted from this evening. But not the same as when I reached Ama's house. Now we've read the note, we can't ignore it. We have a dilemma. The thought of working for our enemy, The Grandfather, makes me sick to my stomach, but we must work to protect the whole of our worldwide secret Leapling community. Imagine if the writer of the note told the world about our Gift? Life would never be the same again.

We're The Infinites. We must rise to the challenge.

Chapter 05:00

GRANDMA IS NOT HERSELF

I leap back to the flat and arrive at 10 p.m. exactly. It's a relief to be back in 2022, real time, the absolute present. It's pitch black, Grandma's obviously not back from her cleaning job yet. Which is odd, since I thought she'd be back by 8 p.m. I can never keep track of her multiple shifts; they seem to change on a weekly basis. I turn on the lights in the sitting room and adjoining kitchen. The fish stew and rice are still on top of the cooker where I left them. Maybe she went to church for all-night prayer. I decide to leave them be for the time being and get ready for bed. If she's not back by the time I've cleaned my teeth, I'll put them in the fridge.

I click-clack the sofa bed so it flattens out and open the door to Grandma's bedroom to get my sheet and duvet from the top of her wardrobe in the far left-hand corner of the room. As I do this, there's a sudden movement beside the bed which makes me jump. I see the faint outline of a small man in a suit and top hat and my heart almost leaps out of my chest with shock. It has to be The Grandfather! But before I have time to react, I notice he's supporting a small, round figure much, much smaller than Millennia. Who can it be? It LOOKS like a woman. The figure is wearing something on her head. Slowly they both come into focus and the outlines become solid. I focus on the woman, hoping she's not who I think she is but knowing the worst has already happened.

The Grandfather has kidnapped Grandma!

It takes more than a few seconds for me to process this. Several thoughts are darting through my brain at the same time: if he's kidnapped Grandma, why has he brought her to the flat? So that I can see she's alive? If he wants money, we don't have any, so what's his motive? Does it have anything to do with the note he gave us in 1880? What can I use to attack him without leaving the room?

While I'm thinking this, The Grandfather virtually drops Grandma into her bedside chair. She looks grey with exhaustion, her blue-green zigzag headtie unravelling like it's alive. It falls onto the floor, revealing her cropped grey hair. Seeing her so vulnerable gives me courage.

'What are you doing here? Get out!'

'Not a polite way to greet your elders,' says The Grandfather, narrowing his grey eyes at me. 'Even if you've seen too much of me this evening, don't forget your manners!'

'What have you done with Grandma?'

'Providing an excellent service, as usual.'

'What do you mean?'

'Ask your grandma. She has a very lively tongue.'

I look at Grandma but she doesn't look very lively at all. She seems half dead when she looks up at The Grandfather.

'Please, I beg. Leave me with Elle.' Her voice is almost a whisper.

'You better make her a strong tea. Top cupboard in the—'

'Don't tell me what to do, I know where it is. You heard Grandma, get out!'

The Grandfather bows and disappears into thin air.

Thank goodness he's gone. He obviously hadn't kidnapped Grandma but I don't like it one bit. I sit on the bed next to her.

'Grandma, what's happening?'

'Make me tea. And bring biscuit.'

I rush into the kitchen to put the kettle on and fetch Grandma her favourite oat biscuits. She doesn't eat many sweet things – she says lots of savoury foods are sweet, meaning tasty – but her soft spot is biscuits. I put some on a plate and take them into the bedroom. Grandma never eats biscuits straight out of the packet, she likes to do things properly. But right now, she looks like she hasn't got the strength to eat.

Once Grandma has her tea she slowly begins to come back to life. It's the strongest I've ever made it and I put two sugars in. I watch her intently, desperate to ask lots of questions but knowing she needs time to recover. Between sips of her drink, she begins to speak.

'Elle, how are you?'

'I'm fine, Grandma. But I'm worried about you.'

'I am tired but not dead. It has not yet come to pass.'

'Grandma, what are you saying?'

'Ah-ah! What did I tell you this morning? I have had a good life. We all die. Death is part of life. Without death we would not breathe. Too much people.'

I frown. Grandma talking about death has made me sad but also it doesn't make sense. She didn't say anything at all to me this morning. She was asleep when I left for school and had gone to work when I got back to cook the stew. The only time we've spoken today is when she phoned on her Chronophone to say have a dance on me. She must have dreamt our earlier conversation and is mixing that up with reality. Again, I worry about her memory but I have to ask the question.

'Grandma, are you going to die?'

She dunks a biscuit in her mug and takes a big bite. 'Yes, but not now.'

'Do you know when?'

'Elle! We discussed this before. But I am ready when the time comes. Not like him. He did not repent his sins-o!' She shakes her head.

'Who? The Grandfather?'

She looks at me as if I'm 2-leap. 'With your good brain, why can you not reason?' Then she notes my puzzled expression and adds, 'Sorry. It is Grandma who cannot reason.'

I'm frightened when she says this. Maybe there really is something wrong with her. But I try not to show it.

'Grandma, you're tired. If you have a good sleep, you'll feel better in the morning.'

She suddenly stiffens in her chair, eyes wide. 'That is it! I am forgetting myself. Which one are you? From the present or the future?'

'From now. It's me, Elle.'

'My Elle Bíbi-Imbelé!' Grandma sounds almost like her old self. 'How was the party?'

'Good,' I say, knowing it's not the full truth, but I can't tell Grandma everything that happened tonight. We're both too exhausted for that.

'Did you cook stew?'

'Yes, Grandma. Would you like me to warm some?'

'Give me small-small. And jellof it.'

Grandma means mix the stew into the plain white boiled rice so it's red and flavoured like jellof rice. Not as good as cooking the rice with stew from scratch but it still tastes good.

When it's ready, Grandma says a short prayer over the food and eats slowly, with effort, but I can tell she's enjoying it. I let her eat in silence whilst I wash up and put the remaining food in the fridge. Then I get ready for bed. It's been a long day.

But when I finally get into bed, my mind starts racing, asking all the questions I couldn't ask Grandma because she was so weak. Why was she leaping with The Grandfather? Where did they go? How does she know an arch criminal in the first place? How long has this been going on? And on top of that, other questions that might be related. Why did The Grandfather really give me and Big Ben the mysterious note? Does Grandma know about that? MC^2 called Grandma a dark horse. Maybe she really has got hidden talents and that's why she keeps so many secrets. Maybe Grandma is more complicated than I ever imagined.

Chapter 06:00

STRENGTH TRAINING

It's the day after Halloween, Tuesday the 1st of November. I barely slept at all but it's cross country first lesson so at least I don't have to concentrate too much. I'm more mentally tired than physically. Cross country at Intercalary International isn't what it says it is. It's as many times round the school field as you can run in 40 minutes. Most of the class walk some of the way since you have to be quite fit to run for 40 minutes. Big Ben and I love it; it's our strength training. I used to think strength in running meant having big muscles but it actually means having the power to run hard for longer. It's very different to sprinting.

It's a damp, windy morning that smells like earth, the autumn leaves bright yellow, red and gold blowing all over the field; they look beautiful but I hope the ground's not too slippery. Big Ben and I set off at the front like we always do. He's super fit because he's been doing football and athletics training for a year now. His favourite event is the 800 metres and in the winter he does lots of cross country, sometimes up hills but often on pavements in the evenings.

I'm training for the indoor pentathlon, which is five events: 60-metre hurdles, long jump, high jump, shot put and 800 metres. Not to be confused with the modern pentathlon, which involves shooting and swimming. Mr Branch, my athletics coach, says the pentathlon is a great way to add variety to my training and doing a longer race will increase my strength.

As I get into my stride, I focus on my breath and making sure my shoulders are relaxed rather than letting my mind wander. GMT's been teaching us mindfulness meditation. 'Guys,' she says, 'it's not enough to be physically fit; you have to be mentally fit too.' Mindfulness means being alert to the present moment rather than focusing too much on the past and the future. Quite a challenge for us Leaplings with The Gift!

Once we've got into our stride and there's a big gap between us and the others, I tell Big Ben about The Grandfather and Grandma. He stumbles with surprise.

'Does Grandma know about The Vicious Circle and the note?'

'I don't know. She wouldn't tell me anything.'

'Maybe he really is helping her leap.'

'BB, I don't trust him an inch. It can't be coincidence that he gave us the note last night AND leapt with Grandma.'

'But it could be,' says Big Ben. 'Just because it happened around the same time doesn't mean it's connected. No one's 100% evil.'

We're quiet for a bit when we lap some of our classmates,

then pick up from where we left off: the note and the threat to tell the world about The Gift.

'Any ideas who wrote it?' I say.

Big Ben's brilliant at working things out logically. And he enjoys problem solving. He already started the process of elimination last night.

'They don't want money, they want a job.'

I nod as I run. 'Yes. Usually notes like that ask for money. But money doesn't motivate this person. They just want power.'

The sun's come out and I feel sweat prickling my armpits. We lap some more of our classmates and make sure we're clear of them before we continue the conversation. Then we slow down a bit; usually we don't talk and run at the same time, it's far too tiring.

'They said Chrono of Crime. Why would they use that phrase unless they were a member of The Vicious Circle?' I say.

I remind Big Ben about the time I infiltrated one of their meetings in disguise and that's how The Grandfather opened the gathering: 'Chrono of crime, thieves of time, let us commence!'

Big Ben frowns. 'Nona, Meridian and The Grandfather all hate Millennia. But would they—'

'Millennia – who's that?' says Jake, running up beside us.

Maria joins him shortly afterwards and we all slow down to a jog. I'm not going to answer Jake – he doesn't know about The Infinites – but he's not letting it go.

'Come on, spill the beans. I know something's up. You're usually miles ahead.'

I'm quite impressed Jake's noticed. He IS clever, even though he hides it by being cheeky. But Maria isn't interested in who Millennia might be.

'Do you two fancy work experience in 2050? Or have you got something sorted? Jake and I have a day at E-College-E next week. You and Big Ben could come, there's a few places left.'

'We haven't finalised anything yet,' I say. 'And thanks for the thought, but no.' I'm thinking about our latest task. I find it hard to concentrate on more than one thing at a time. 'We're too busy.'

'We could train at the Music, Maths and Movement School track afterwards. Your high jump's really coming on, Elle.'

Maria's a high-jump champion and has been helping with my technique for the pentathlon. People always try to bribe me with athletics. Occasionally it works but not this time. The note is too important. Our whole way of life is at stake.

'Busy with what?' asks Jake.

I make a snap decision. Big Ben and I haven't made much progress. Maybe Jake or Maria can help. We don't have to tell them too much detail. I take a deep breath.

'OK,' I say, 'but this is top secret. What would you do if someone threatened to break The Oath? Publicly.'

Jake stops running and his mouth drops open. 'You serious? Easy. Kill them.' He starts running again, catching up with us.

Now my mouth's a capital O. 'You ARE joking?'

'Yes, I'm joking,' replies Jake. 'Kind of. Haven't we been taught since birth that's the worst thing a Leapling or Annual could do? Private's frowned on, but making it public? Absolute no-no!'

'Jake's right,' adds Maria. 'It would be the ultimate betrayal.'

'Who's this SOMEONE?' Jake looks around the field as if it's one of our class.

'We don't know. There was a note,' says Big Ben, and I frown at him. I didn't want to give away too much information.

'What did it say?'

'It won't make sense,' I say, 'unless we tell you a whole load of stuff and we can't tell you here. You'll have to drop round my flat after school.'

'OK,' they say.

The four of us continue running round the field. I'm fit, but I'm running like I've got lead in my legs at the thought of the task ahead. We're only 14 years old. Are we up to the job?

Chapter 07:00

MILLENNIA'S MALEVOLENT MILLENNIALS

It's 7 p.m. Jake and Maria have left the flat, open-mouthed but their lips are sealed. Big Ben and I didn't tell them everything, but we showed them the note and told them to help us if they had any ideas.

This evening, Big Ben has flying lessons in Portia's Porsche. He's already been out on a few trips without me and has made some progress. Not that he needs much tuition; he's a natural handling futuristic supercars. As he says, he's only crashed once and that was the first time he flew Season's Ferrari Forever.

Portia arrives at my flat just after 7 p.m. and I can tell as soon as she walks through the door that something's up because her usually spiky peacock hair is even wilder than usual. She always ruffles her hair when she's thinking hard about something. But I sense she's trying to rein in her emotions.

'You two ready?'

'I didn't know I was coming,' I say.

'I need to speak to both of you. And I feel safer in the car. Season checked it for bugs last night. No hidden microphones or cameras.'

I'm anxious about what she just said and dying to know what's up but Portia hates to be rushed. She'll let us know soon enough. Big Ben and I grab our bags and the three of us walk out into the night. This time of year is ideal, as it's dark. We only have to drive a couple of streets away to the industrial area, where we can take off. Her silver Porsche is parked across the road.

We get in, Big Ben in the driver's seat on the right, Portia beside him and me on the back seat behind Portia. I wedge myself in with the heavy blanket she keeps there for the odd time she sleeps overnight in the car, more for comfort than warmth. It's a bit naughty Big Ben taking the wheel; it's not legal to drive in 2022 until you're 17 and he's still only 14 but we'll be up in the air in the future in less than a minute. After 2040, you can drive legally at 14.

When Portia taps in the destination, date and time – no fixed location: Tuesday 1 November 2050: 19:00 – I notice her hand is shaking. It's a smooth take-off but I still feel sick when it angles into the air. I pop a strawberry leap sweet into my mouth and try to relax. But it's hard to relax as we accelerate through time and space. Tonight, for some reason, there's loads of air traffic in 2050, headlights all over the night sky. It's very windy too, the kind of gusts you get before a winter storm. Big Ben's swerving all over the place. It's like being in a computer game, except it's real.

'Trust the programme,' says Portia. 'If you go by instinct, we'll go upside-down!'

'Logical,' says Big Ben.

That's not very reassuring. What if the programme goes wrong? But I daren't voice that aloud in case I somehow make it real. It's the hardest flight I've experienced because the first part is so quiet there's nothing to distract me from the nausea and fear. On top of that, Portia is jumpy. According to Big Ben, she usually compliments him on his driving but tonight she's critical. Whatever it is, Portia's a time-bomb ready to go off.

'Guys, bad news,' she says.

I take a deep breath. 'Everyone knows about Leaplings?'

'No. I've been demoted!'

'How?' asks Big Ben. 'Yesterday you were promoted to Two. Are you One again?'

'No. But Millennia called me and Destiny to an emergency meeting today with the Elders. It's about the recruitment of techy teens for world domination: Millennia's Millennials. She said I've failed at the job. Been too slow. And guess who she's put in charge?'

'Destiny,' we say at exactly the same time.

'I was totally humiliated. Millennia said Destiny got the job done in one hour twenty! Destiny smirked her head off. But Millennia has a point. You all know it's been impossible for me to get teens who'd be double agents too. I couldn't find anyone I could trust.'

Big Ben nods as he swerves to miss a maxi-mini. 'How many teens did Destiny recruit?'

'Three. Code names Taurus, Gemini and Scorpio.'

'Were they at the meeting?'

'No. Millennia never wants to meet them. She likes to pretend she doesn't mix with petty criminals, remember. Then if they're arrested, she can play innocent.'

Something's niggling at me. 'Has Millennia guessed you're working for us?' I ask.

Portia sighs so deeply her whole body shudders. Yet she seems calmer, as if sharing this with us fellow Infinites is making her feel better.

'That's what I'm worried about. It all seems so sudden. I used to be Millennia's favourite. She loved me to chaperone her in the Porsche when The Grandfather couldn't luggage her. It's like she switched on Halloween. Destiny's the favourite now, she's— WATCH OUT!'

Big Ben swerves to miss a convoy of lorries. I don't think I can cope with much more of this. Too much traffic, air turbulence and bad news all at once.

'Best I take over from here,' says Portia.

Big Ben shakes his head. 'I want to drive!'

'You're doing OK,' agrees Portia, 'but it's too busy. Get in the back with Elle.'

'Portia's right, BB,' I say. 'We have to follow the ground rules.'

I say this because as much as Big Ben wants to continue driving, he respects the rules Portia set up when they started lessons. Rule number 1 was to follow Portia's instructions exactly; rule number 5 was to sit in the back when not driving. It would be impossible for Big Ben to sit in the passenger seat and not try to drive. I remind him of the rules because I want him to feel respected and avoid having a meltdown from the unexpected change of plan. As Big Ben lowers his seat completely and shuffles into the one behind, Portia slides across to the driver's seat.

It's just as well they swapped; things go from bad to worse.

The car starts lurching up and down, making strange grunting noises like it's kangaroo petrol. But it can't be kangaroo petrol: Portia's Porsche is an eco-friendly supercar that runs on wind and rain. Something's not right.

'What's happening?' I say.

'Interference!' replies Portia, pressing several buttons in quick succession.

'From the weather?'

'No. Something wrong with the controls. It's not letting me override the programme. We're heading north-west.'

'Wales?'

'No, it's . . . what? A smiley face on the speedometer? Someone's idea of a—'

'Land the car!' says Big Ben.

'I would if I could. But there's no land to land on any more, only sea. Brace yourselves, guys – we're heading for Iceland!'

∞

We land on a flat piece of land that look-s like the surface of the moon, all grey and cratered except for a range of mountains in the distance, but the car doesn't stop straight away. It continues in a straight line, gradually decelerating. I struggle to open an orange leap sweet and Big Ben has to help me. He's lucky – he doesn't get leapsick or carsick ever. The citrus flavour makes me feel instantly better but still rubbish.

'Look, there's people,' says Big Ben, looking outside his window. 'I think they want a lift.'

I can't cope with looking out of his window right now. All my energy is going into not vomiting all over the car. But I wonder who on earth would be thumbing a lift in Iceland, at night, in the middle of nowhere.

'Trouble ahead!' says Portia, trying to sound calm. 'Elle, Big Ben, blanket drill! Now!'

Portia's Porsche isn't the smallest of models but it certainly isn't big enough for us to stretch out, especially Big Ben. However, we know what blanket drill means: lie down and don't look like someone hiding under a blanket! The Infinites have done emergency training with MC^2 for moments like this. In a matter of seconds, the back seat looks totally uninhabited. But under the blanket, Big Ben and I hold our breaths, wondering what danger lies ahead. We can't see anything but we'll have to listen hard in case we have to split-second leap away to safety. It can't be a border control. Maybe it's the police. I hope it's still 2050; if it's before flying cars were the norm, we'll have a lot of explaining to do.

The car slows down to a halt and Portia unwinds her window.

'Destiny!' she says. 'It was you all the time. Had my suspicions.'

'You give me too much credit,' replies a teen girl voice with a slight accent. 'I work with words not tech. Taurus was the mastermind; Gemini reset your car; Scorpio directed it. Now it is mindless as a drone. They are the brain.'

'Impressive work,' replies Portia. 'But now you've had your fun, I need to get home.'

'Correction. WE need to get home. You will give the four of us a lift in your Porsche.'

'Correction. I will fly home alone. You and your troublesome techs will leap home in a Chrono. One does not give orders to Two.'

I move ever so slightly under the blanket. I was never good at keeping still and it's torture listening to this conversation but not being able to see it.

'True,' replies Destiny, 'but Taurus, Gemini and Scorpio are Annuals. It was exhausting for me to luggage them here. I need a lift back. If Millennia hears you refused to cooperate—'

'I'm busy. You interrupted an urgent job,' says Portia, then her voice softens a bit as the threat of Millennia sinks in. 'I'll come back for you when I'm finished.'

'And how long will that take? Let me assist you. I use my Leapling skills to the max. I can do more work in a minute than you can do in a month. Of course, you could do your job in slow motion real time and still leap back to this moment to drive us, but you don't want to. You cannot hide it: if looks could kill, Destiny is dead.' She pauses. 'You're shivering, Portia. Too cold for you here in Iceland, in 2050?' Laughter in the background. 'Maybe you should use your blanket.' Silence. Oh my Chrono, maybe she's guessed that we're hidden here. But she continues speaking. 'I for one am disappointed with the lack of ice. Global warming has ruined my view.'

'Why are you here?'

58

There's a long pause, then the voice of a teenage boy. 'Sightseeing.'

'The Northern Lights are quite spectacular at this time of year,' says Destiny, 'but Taurus is not telling the whole truth. Destiny is looking for a mid-century base away from people. Snow is fine but I detest rain. Too much of the world is flooded and overcrowded.'

'Go to Mars then!'

'I could leap anywhere in the universe and I have access to the technology to survive but' – she pauses for dramatic effect – 'my ambitions are here on Earth.'

'And what are your ambitions, exactly?' Portia can't keep the sarcasm out of her voice.

'The same as Millennia's: world domination,' replies Destiny. 'And now, Portia, since I suspect your urgent job is a work of fiction, I'm asking you again to drive us back to London.'

Time to leap. Definitely time to leap. I've leapt across time on so many occasions now but I've never leapt across so much space. Neither has Big Ben. But we can't remain here. If we do, Destiny will know that Portia's a double agent and I hate to imagine how Millennia would punish her. Big Ben and I somehow manage to hold hands under the blanket and concentrate for all we're worth on my flat, 8 p.m., the 1st of November 2022. In the case of an emergency like now, when we can't communicate aloud, we always leap back to the original destination the hour after we left.

In a nanosecond we're no longer in Iceland and I relax, knowing that Portia is safe. This helps with what is the most challenging leap of my life. It seems to go on forever and if it weren't for Big Ben holding firmly onto both hands, I would give up and drop into the middle of the sea without a trace. But I don't give up; we give each other strength. We maintain our grip on each other and our destination point and eventually there is no longer the feeling of being tossed around in a tumble drier; it's more like a normal leap through time, with the tiny white numbers dotted against the night sky until there is a sense of landing and the numbers slowing until they come to a stop.

We've landed in the middle of my kitchen. I check the time and date on my Chronophone before projectile vomiting all over the floor. I've been holding it in for a very long time. And even though I feel weak from the leap and the nausea and the strange experience of witnessing Portia and Destiny and her techy teen team from under the blanket, I feel exhilarated too. We've learnt stuff that could be useful in the future: Destiny is super-ambitious; Taurus, Gemini and Scorpio are supertalented; and Big Ben and I just leapt across time and a continent. If we can do that, we can achieve anything.

Chapter 08:00

MOON & SONS

It's Wednesday after school and it's all happening. The Infinites just had part one of an emergency meeting at Ama's games room in 2050; Big Ben got a text from The Grandfather on his Chronophone!

> Leap to Moon & Sons, Clerkenwell, London at 6 p.m.
> on the 29th of February 1888. The second note is here.

The 29th of February means a leap day; I wonder if that's significant. I'm glad there's another note. Big Ben and I haven't made any more progress deciphering the first one and time is ticking. It's essential we find out who wants to tell the world Leaplings can leap through time. Maybe the second note will give us more of a clue.

Me, Big Ben and GMT leap to an alleyway close to The Grandfather's shop in case anyone sees us leaping, then turn into Clerkenwell. GMT volunteered to accompany us on this mission as she's been here before so many times with MC². In her past life, Moon & Sons was one of their favourite haunts. Clerkenwell has lots of dilapidated bookshops but we pass several clockshops on the way too. The Grandfather has plenty of competition.

Eventually we come to a smart, black-painted wooden shop-front that says Jeweller: Moon & Sons: Watchmaker with 22 above it. 22 must be the number of the shop. The two large glass windows either side are crammed full of pocket watches and jewellery. The dark polished door is closed and there appear to be flickering lights inside the shop. The brass door knocker is an elaborate sun and moon design. We knock on the door at exactly 6 o'clock.

The door creaks open and a short man with deathly white skin, black hair streaked with grey slicked to his head, and wearing peculiar goggles opens it. His eyes are distorted through his specialised glasses but they're an unmistakable slate grey. This is the middle-aged 1888 version of The Grandfather!

'Sorry, we are . . . oh, it's you. I suppose you had better come in. But YOU,' gesturing towards GMT, 'stay outside or I'll call the law.'

'That's not fair. You got your watches back,' I say, before I can stop myself.

'This is MY shop and I make the rules. Do not make this tedious for me; the déjà vu is already nauseating. Elle and Big Ben, if you hesitate any longer I will be forced to act on my threat.'

We have no choice but to walk into the shop, leaving GMT outside. Frankly, she looks relieved, but we tell her to wait so we can all leap back together to part two of our emergency meeting. The 1888 Grandfather closes the door and locks it. If we need to leave at any time, we're going to have to leap.

It takes a second or two to take in the candlelit interior. There's a long counter made of dark wood, glass cases full of gold and silver chains, gleaming and glistening stones embedded in necklaces and chunky black chokers. I'm a bit overawed by the sensory overload. Although I find sparkly things beautiful, I have to squint and look sideways to cope with lots of them. On top of the visuals, there's a tick-tock rhythm coming from the left-hand corner. A tall oak grandfather clock with a weak–strong heartbeat. I'm mesmerised by it, like it's actually alive. Big Ben's drawn to it too. We've read about them but never seen one in real life. Our host, on the other hand, is unimpressed with absolutely everything.

'I am 36 years of age and have already lived a lifetime. I remember this scene from when I was 14 years old. At that age, I played the leading role and despised my senior self; now I have the indignity of being in the supporting role. I no longer possess the vitality to change the script. Therefore, I hand you over to my misspent youth.' He pauses. 'Junior!'

The teen version of The Grandfather appears from a door to the right. He too is wearing the strange goggles. They must use them to look at the tiny parts of the watches.

'Your friends have arrived,' says 1888, and I wince at the word friends even though he's being sarcastic. We couldn't be more the opposite of friends. And now I have the added anxiety that The Grandfather junior was leaping with Grandma, I'm even more suspicious of him. Before we left, MC² reminded us of Grandma's advice: know thine enemy. 'Ask lots of questions, Leaps. Even spit you think is trivial,' he said. Now we're here, though, I can't think of anything to say. The flickering candle-light, sparkling jewels and ticking clocks are making me queasy like I'm leaping; it's difficult to think, let alone speak. But Big Ben, thankfully, has a question for 1888.

'Are you Mr Moon?' he says.

'No. We do not descend from Moon. Our great-grandfather had an odd sense of humour. The business name stuck. But he did not predict that in future generations he would have more than one version of the same son running the family business.'

'It's all down to me; I got all the talent. He don't do nothing. Good at business, bad at working,' says the teen.

'Respect your elders.'

'Only if they earn it.'

'It is at this point,' says 1888, 'that my 3-leap daughter, Rosalind, enters the scene to further undermine my authority.'

At that exact moment, a small but strong-looking girl with cat-green eyes, black pigtails coiled round the back of her head, and wearing a white pinafore dress bursts into the shop. She is so full of energy, I imagine sparks bouncing off her.

'Papa, where is the birthday gift you promised me?'

'My dear Rosalind, it is hidden and your task is to find it.'

'Easy-peasy!' says Rosalind and begins pulling out tiny drawers left, right and centre with more skill than any thief. In less than a minute the entire shop is ransacked and she sits on the floor out of breath. Then she springs up again.

'Why, of course!' she says and bounds towards the grandfather clock, opens the door and reaches inside like she's pulling out its heart. 'What's this?'

She pulls out a black envelope and I silently gasp. It's identical to the one that contained the first note.

'Not for your eyes, Rosalind,' says The Grandfather teen, but she's already tearing it open and reading the contents out loud.

Search my area!
Who am I?
Ask r, The Squared
and their best friend, Pi.

She looks at her father. 'Well, that's a ridiculous clue. I give up. I want my present now!' Then she narrows her eyes at me and Big Ben. 'Who are you? Are you friends with Junior? Can you time travel? I'm brilliant at it but Papa tries to stop me. He's so behind the times, he's a dinosaur! Mama can't leap but would love me to have a better life. Imagine having to spend your 3-leap birthday in 1888!' She flings the envelope and note on the floor and flounces out of the room.

1888 raises his voice as if making an announcement. 'And now the finale in which I prove myself to be, contrary to Rosalind's opinion, open to future ideas.'

'Ha!' says The Grandfather teen. 'Only in business. You lost your touch at everything else years ago. Leave the complicated stuff to me.' He turns to us. 'Elle, take the note. Report back to me as soon as you know who wrote it.'

I take a deep breath to combat the nausea from the sensory overload, squat down to pick up the discarded papers, slip the slightly crumpled note back in the black envelope and put it into my rucksack. Something's been niggling at me about Moon & Sons. Finally, I have a question. It's an effort to speak when I feel so overwhelmed but my curiosity overrides it.

'Sir,' I say, to make it clear I'm addressing 1888 rather than the evil teen, 'do you teach your daughter, Rosalind, to make and mend watches?'

'I do,' he replies, 'and she would be excellent if she could only sit still longer than five minutes.'

'If Rosalind got good, and inherited the business, would you change the sign to Moon & Daughter?'

1888 frowns as if deep in thought for several seconds. Then his face brightens and even shows a little colour.

'Yes. Indeed I would,' he says.

'No need,' says The Grandfather teen. 'Rosalind don't care about keeping time; just leaping through it. But Rosalind's daughter; now she's a different kettle of fish altogether.'

The Grandfather senior frowns with distaste but The Grandfather junior smiles like a grimace. The smile says: I leap, I take risks and I know what happens in the future. Big Ben and I know who he's talking about. Rosalind will grow up to have a daughter who wants to know EVERYTHING about time. Who wants to use that knowledge to gain power and prestige. She will be called Millennia.

Chapter 09:00

BRAINBUZZ

B ack at the 2050 meeting, I realise I have another text. It's from Jake.

Got idea about that note. Let's talk!

'It really is all happening,' I say as Big Ben and I fill the other Infinites in on all the details from what just happened in 1888. 'We've got another note and Jake has an idea about the first one. We had to tell him and Maria, it's such a serious threat. Shall I tell him to leap here?'

Kwesi gives a small nod but MC^2 narrows his eyes. 'Jake's the Leap from your school?'

'Yes,' I reply. 'They overheard our conversation about the first note so Big Ben and I showed it to them back at my flat. I'm sure we can trust them.'

MC^2 turns to Kwesi. 'You safe about them coming to your yard?'

Kwesi nods and signs rapidly in his own style.

'OK, Elle,' says MC². 'Invite him. And Maria. We don't have Coleridge today cos brother's got a big-time composition deadline. We need all the help we can get. You an' Big Ben are running this show. Chair the meet but shift your feet. We gotta get results fast.'

At that precise moment, Robot enters the room.

'Dinner is served. It is beanfeast, an imaginative blend of colours, flavours and textures to suit every palate. Please assemble in the dining-room.'

∞

Ama's dining room is a massive white room next to the kitchen. Robot has served dinner in huge, heaped bowls in the middle of the long black table and we've all helped ourselves. Like most people in the future, Ama's family only eat meat once a week, in their case on a Sunday because they're Christian. Kind of. So this dinner is totally vegan, a vibrant range of colours and smells. Thank goodness I have my colour-coolers on me. I wear them so that I'm not overwhelmed by the bright and contrasting colours of food. At the moment they're set similar to strong sunglasses; I can see the colours but in muted shades.

'The note's a hoax,' says Jake, stuffing his face full of something that looks like chicken nuggets but is made out of borlotti beans. 'How can we make them Midnight if we don't know who they are? What are they getting out of this? They don't want money.' He chews a bit. 'They're definitely having a laugh.'

'But if it's a hoax,' I reply, 'why did they go to so much trouble making the note, delivering it at a specific time AND sending a second one? It doesn't make sense.'

Big Ben clears his throat and pauses a few seconds. 'They want power, not money.'

'They certainly have power over us,' I agree. 'And they always deliver to The Grandfather. Why not Millennia? We have to solve this.'

Maria waves her arms around. 'You have to tell me and Jake more. Who is The Grandfather? Who is Millennia?'

'First things first,' says MC². 'We ain't seen the second note yet. Show us, Elle.'

I take it out of my bag and squash it flat on the table. It's the same newspaper collage style. Everyone strains to look at it as I read it out loud for Big Ben. As I do so, I can hear Rosalind's commanding voice echoing in my head.

Search my area!
Who am I?
Ask r, The Squared
and their best friend, Pi.

'OK, so who's r?' asks Maria. 'If we're doing it in order, we should start with that.'

MC² gives Maria a raised eyebrow look that says 'You only just joined the meeting, don't try to take over'. But it doesn't work; Maria's too feisty to keep quiet.

'Why don't we have a brainbuzz?' she says. 'We write down all the ideas, even the bad ones. Then we'll get to the truth.'

'Good idea,' I say, standing up from the table. It's my job to chair the meeting. I want to do a good job.

'I agree,' says Ama, who's been busy keeping an eye on Robot in the kitchen until now. 'Use our collective intelligence. Like ants.'

'Ants are stupid,' says Jake, and Maria rolls her eyes.

'Robot!' calls Ama, 'keep track of the brainbuzz, please! And take minutes of the meeting.'

'Does that mean time it?' says Big Ben.

'No. Just note important stuff and what we decide to do.'

Robot appears from the kitchen and projects the word BRAINBUZZ onto the blank wall behind us. As we move our chairs to face it and voice our ideas, the wall starts to fill up, colour-coded to differentiate between us. My contributions are red.

'Does anyone have any idea who's writing these notes?' I ask. There's a long silence. 'We have to be open to every possibility at this stage; even ideas that may seem unlikely could lead us to the truth. Jake says it's someone who's having a laugh. Big Ben says someone who wants power. I think it's someone who wants attention.'

'What do you mean, exactly?' It's Portia. She's been unusually quiet this evening.

'I mean' – I think for a little – 'that they want us to take notice of them. They want to feel important. And they think they can run The Vicious Circle.'

70

'Well, it's not me,' says Portia, going red. 'I can't think of anything worse.'

'Shall we turn to the second note?' I say. 'It says "Ask r". Any ideas who r might be? Who would make their initial lower case?'

'What does that mean?' asks Big Ben, scraping his plate clean of blackeye bean stew that even Grandma would be proud of.

'People usually write their initials with a capital letter. This is a small r. It must be someone unconventional.' I pause. 'Rosalind!'

'The Grandfather's daughter is Rosalind. And she FOUND the note in the grandfather clock.'

'Yes, BB. And she's a Leapling too. She's young but she boasted about time-travelling. Maybe she knows something.'

'Before you start,' says MC², 'it ain't me neither. The Squared is innocent.'

'We trust you,' I say, 'but The Squared is mentioned in the note. Maybe you know something but don't know it's relevant.'

MC² shrugs but looks annoyed. Kwesi signs something to him and he seems to relax a bit. GMT seems totally absorbed in her beancakes. We're not making much progress.

Big Ben is shaking his head. 'We didn't start from the beginning. We have to search my area. Is it the area around Moon & Sons in 1888? We leapt back here too quick.'

He helps himself to something that looks like brown rice to accompany his third helping of blackeye bean stew. I must get the recipe from Ama. It really is delicious.

'I think we should ask pi,' says Jake. 'I fancy some pie myself. Can Robot rustle up some cherry pie for pudding?'

'Very funny, not,' says Maria.

Big Ben frowns. 'Read the note out loud again.'

As I do, he closes his eyes. Big Ben always does this when he's solving a maths problem. I wonder what he'll come up with this time. He opens his eyes.

'I know who it is,' he says.

'Who?' we say, almost in unison.

'The Vicious Circle!'

'Explain, bro,' says MC^2 with a sigh of relief. I think he's glad Big Ben didn't say it was him.

'The clue said search my AREA. It mentioned r and The Squared and pi. Pi is the Greek letter you use to work out the area of a circle: π. The area of a circle is pi multiplied by the radius, r, squared: πr^2.'

'Like a cryptic crossword clue?' I say.

'No. Like a maths problem. But it can't be just any circle. In this case, it has to be The Vicious Circle. Elle and I thought it was likely after the first note; now we have definite proof.'

'You're brilliant, BB.' I smile. 'You worked it out!'

Kwesi thumbs-up to Big Ben and signs rapidly; MC^2 translates.

'Brother says you talk good sense. But how can the whole Vicious Circle wanna be Midnight? That's 12 folks and one of them's Millennia. She don't need to be leader; she's already top dog.'

I cut in. 'I think BB's right. But search my area means we have to search The Vicious Circle itself. It said "Who am I", not "Who are we". The writer of the notes is a MEMBER of The Vicious Circle.'

Everyone looks at Portia; she looks down. There's an awkward silence, only broken by Maria's question.

'You can't invite me and Jake to your meeting and not tell us anything. Who and what is The Vicious Circle?'

'Portia,' I say, 'you'll have to fill them in. And we all need an update after what's happened recently.'

While Portia says who's who, especially Ten, Eleven and Twelve, the Elders, Ama instructs Robot to show us a diagram of all the members of the evil gang. It looks something like this:

Big Ben rises from his seat in excitement. 'Elle,' he says, 'the numbers are in a circle like they're real people. It doesn't matter that I can't read the words.'

He's right. The digits have more impact than the words. The

Vicious Circle model themselves on a traditional clock face. Seeing them sitting in formation makes my heart pound in my chest.

Big Ben sits down again to finish his stew and addresses the whole table.

'We've met Destiny and Portia and Sonos and Chronos,' he says, 'and Nona and Meridian and The Grandfather and Millennia. That's 8 out of 12, two thirds of the whole gang.'

'Not properly,' I correct him. 'You and I SAW Destiny at the Beat Battle and HEARD Destiny under the blanket in Portia's car. We don't really know who she is. And we only heard Sonos and Chronos rapping. I saw them at The Vicious Circle meeting but they didn't say anything. What are they like, Portia?'

She shrugs her shoulders. 'Ambitious. But more about their music than in The Vicious Circle. I doubt they want to run things.'

'What about this Destiny?' says MC^2. 'She ain't scared of ambition.'

'You're right there,' say Portia. 'She loved taking my job and I wouldn't be surprised if she thought she deserved more promotion up The Circle. But she seems totally in awe of Millennia. I don't think she wants HER position.'

'What about Portia?' asks Maria. 'Or aren't we allowed to discuss her?'

I look at Kwesi, MC^2 and GMT, not sure what to do. How can we discuss Portia when she's right in front of us?

Kwesi signs and it's clear what he means; Portia must wait outside.

GMT explains. 'Portia, it has to be done. It's what folks do when there's a conflict of interests. We all trust that you're on our side, but as you work for us AND are a member of The Vicious Circle, we have to consider you as a suspect, however unlikely it is. It won't take long.'

I can see by the way Portia leaves the dining room that she's not happy. As soon as she's gone, Maria can't contain herself.

'She's definitely guilty!' she says. 'Did you see how she went red when we hadn't even accused her?'

'That don't mean spit,' says MC². 'She's already bin in Do-Time for theft. I know what it's like. You feel like folks be judging you all of the time.'

'She was in prison?' Jake's eyes almost pop out of his head.

'I trust her,' I say. 'She's a brilliant double agent. She tells us everything Millennia says.'

'I'm not sure,' says Big Ben. 'She should not work on this job. Some of her family are in The Vicious Circle.'

'Only Nine, her aunt Nona, and Portia hates her. Portia's mum and uncle are in prison because of The Vicious Circle. Portia's definitely on our side.'

Kwesi signs and MC² translates. 'Doesn't mean she didn't write the notes. Maybe she wants to take over The VC to reform it.'

We all laugh at the thought.

'Shall I call Portia back in?' I say. 'Are we agreed she should work on this mission?'

Everyone nods except Maria and Big Ben.

'I guess I'll go with the majority,' shrugs Maria.

'What about you, BB?' I ask.

Big Ben pauses several seconds. 'OK.'

'Remember, Leaps,' reminds MC², 'it's you, Elle, and Big Ben on this case. No one else. We're just brainbuzzers.'

'We can't do it without support from The Infinites,' I say. 'And now we have Jake and Maria too, we'll definitely work it out. Let's get Portia back in. She can give us more detail about Five to Eight, the people none of us have properly met yet.'

But Portia seems a bit reluctant to give us information, which is odd. Is she angry because we made her stand outside or is she deliberately hiding something? My trust in Portia starts to waver. It dawns on me that she hasn't ever filled us in on detail about the members of The Vicious Circle. She tells us mainly about what Millennia's up to but The Vicious Circle has 12 members. Surely she knows stuff about the others? Now she has a chance, she's not giving us much to go on. She doesn't know Five or Six's real names, but they're both men: Five is in charge of security and Six is an expert on time and talks nothing but 19th-century trains.

'Is that why Six is called The Trainspotter?' I ask, looking at the circle of names.

'The opposite,' says Portia. 'He HATES trains. But he seems to know all their names and numbers and insists on being called The Trainspotter rather than a rail fan.'

I smile at the irony. 'What about Seven and Eight?'

'Seven's called Romana and Eight's Otto. They're married and work at E-College-E.' She pauses as if she's not sure whether to say more. 'They've donated thousands to The Vicious Circle. I think they're in it for the thrills.'

'Otto's the judge who marked MC² and Kwesi down at the Beat Battle,' I remind everyone. 'And he knows Destiny.'

Maria frowns. 'I'm sure I saw Otto's name on my instructions for next week's work experience.'

Portia turns her hands up to the sky. 'If you all know so much, why are you asking me?'

Maria ignores her. 'Tell us about Ten, Eleven and Twelve again, the Elders.'

As Portia refuses to speak, Big Ben and I do the talking. I'm really worried about Portia now; she's acting so out of character. Sometimes she can sound formal like a teacher when she gets cross but I've never seen her so defensive. I can feel the tension in the room and want to end the meeting. But before I do, there's something I need to know.

'Can everyone tell me who they suspect and why? It will help BB and me in our investigation.'

The heading SUSPECTS is projected onto the wall. Instinctively, everyone communicates in order of seniority within The Infinites, which means Kwesi first.

'The Grandfather,' he signs, 'because he wants to be top dog.'

MC^2 disagrees. 'No, bro. It's gotta be Sonos or Chronos. I see it in their eyes.'

'Definitely Nona,' says GMT. 'She wanted to exit Millennia last year, remember?'

'You next, BB,' I prompt.

Big Ben pauses. 'Otto, because he gave MC^2 and Kwesi a 6 when they deserved a 10!'

'Good man,' says MC^2.

Ama shakes her head. 'I think it's Destiny. Don't forget she hijacked Portia's Porsche to Iceland with you in it! She's ruthless;

she'll do anything to get her own way. What do you think, Portia?'

'Destiny's evil but she doesn't like the limelight. But I know someone who does: The Grandfather,' replies Portia. 'Elle and Big Ben just experienced two of him; he loves drama. I disagree with Kwesi that he wants to be top dog. He's in it for the excitement, not power. The Grandfather probably made the whole thing up cos he wants you to work for him, Elle. Don't trust him. I know how he operates. You should stop the mission.'

'I think it's Destiny,' says Maria. 'She's power crazy.'

'Nah.' Jake shakes his head. 'It's Rosalind. Someone must have got her to plant the note in the clock. Vicious Circle's a red herring.'

He means The Vicious Circle is a distraction put there to take us off track but that would mean BB misinterpreted the note. And I don't think he did.

I take a deep breath. 'So, we have lots of different suspects at this stage: Sonos or Chronos, Nona, Otto and Rosalind have one vote. The Grandfather and Destiny have two. We need more clues and proof before we can narrow it down. At the moment, the only proof we have is that it's a member of The Vicious Circle, so we have to investigate them all, even those with no votes at all.

'The meeting is now closed.' I pause. 'Big Ben and I will investigate each member of The Vicious Circle relating to the notes, starting with Destiny. We'll report back when we can.'

'Good work, Elle,' says MC². 'But tell us who you think wrote the notes.'

'I've got too many ideas in my head,' I say. 'I'll tell you when I narrow it down.'

He nods and I breathe a secret sigh of relief. I do suspect someone but I can't say it out loud because I'm struggling with it emotionally, still trying to process why I've come to that conclusion. I really don't want it to be true but if it is, it's not straightforward. That person is in the room so I can't tell The Infinites; it would cause too much of a storm. I think it's Portia.

Chapter 10:00

COLERIDGE GIVES GRANDMA A GIFT

The kitchen is so full of steam from the bubbling saucepan of moi-moi, water's dripping down the walls. The extractor on the oven isn't working properly and although the windows are open, outside it's catdogs! That's mid-century slang for raining cats and dogs. But it isn't mid-century; we're back in my flat in 2022. I found it difficult to concentrate on Past, Present and Future aka PPF at school today because I've been imagining cooking this special meal. Big Ben's stirring the jellof rice and I'm setting the table. It's 5 p.m.; Coleridge is arriving in half an hour.

Grandma is a bit more like her old self. I've tried quizzing her about leaping with The Grandfather the past few days but she always says, 'Elle, enough!' and purses her lips shut. I desperately want to know what's going on but I don't want to spoil her good mood. Now, she appears from the bedroom squinting in her dressing-gown, her short grey hair on show because she's just woken up. She sucks her teeth.

'Elle, open the door. Let us not grow mushroom for wallpaper!'

She's referring to the terrible mould we used to have before the flat was refurbished. I do as she says, even though I hate the temporary lack of privacy.

'I think the rice is cooked,' says Big Ben.

I taste it with a teaspoon. Perfect! I switch off all the rings. The moi-moi must be ready too; it's been steaming for an hour.

'Who is this your friend coming?' asks Grandma.

'His name is Coleridge, Grandma. He's a composer from the 19th century. His full name is Samuel Coleridge-Taylor.'

As I say it out loud, I wonder how much names make you who you are. If Coleridge's nickname was Taylor, would he be quite so creative?

Someone's knocking on the downstairs door. Surely it must be for us as none of the other occupants are answering it and I gave MC^2 strict instructions not to leap straight to my kitchen in case we were carrying hot food. I slowly walk downstairs to give myself time to adjust to their company and open the door. I was right: Kwesi, MC^2 and Coleridge wearing a black suit, white shirt and black bow tie which contrast dramatically with his untidy afro. He's carrying a small oblong package wrapped in brown paper.

'You're early,' I say to my Infinite friends but not to Coleridge. That would be rude.

'Sorry. Stuff to do in real time,' explains MC^2. 'Text me when you're done. Later, Coleridge!'

Kwesi bumps fists with Coleridge, who follows me up the stairs in silence but it doesn't feel uncomfortable. Like me and

81

Big Ben, he doesn't do small talk. He's shy but back at Ama's on Halloween when he had something important to say, he said it. Grandma is waiting at the door, her eyes narrowed with curiosity. I notice she's put on her purple headtie with gold flecks but still has her dressing-gown on.

'Coleridge. You are welcome.'

'I am honoured, Madam Ifíè,' he responds and gives a little bow.

'Come in,' I say and close the door behind him. 'Do you want a drink?'

Coleridge shakes hands with Big Ben, who is finishing laying the table, sits down at it and puts the package in front of him. He watches me closely as I peel and chop the plantain, salt it and drop each piece into the sizzling oil whilst Grandma gets dressed in her bedroom.

'What's that?' asks Big Ben, pointing to the package.

'A gift for the host,' says Coleridge, but he makes no gesture towards me. The plantain sizzles in the frying pan and I turn it over. The sweet aroma makes my mouth water. Then I drain the moi-moi and open some of the foil to let the steam out. It's when Grandma re-enters the kitchen in her purple gold-flecked wrapper and cream cardigan that Coleridge comes to life. He stands like I used to do in primary school to answer a question and addresses her exclusively.

'Please accept this gift as a token of my gratitude,' he says, his head lowered.

'Thank you. I am very pleased with you,' smiles Grandma, meaning she is pleased to meet Coleridge formally.

'Open it, Grandma!' I say.

She sits at the table next to Coleridge and tears open the package which is tied up with brown string rather than Sellotape. A brown book. A very slim book. Grandma can't read or write but Coleridge doesn't know that.

'Elle, what does it say?'

'*The Song of Hiawatha* by Henry Wadsworth Longfellow.' I open a random page and read out loud.

> 'Two good friends had Hiawatha,
> Singled out from all the others . . .'

'Yes!' says Grandma. 'It is a good poem!'

I frown. 'You know it, Grandma? Did you hear it on the radio?' Grandma smiles mysteriously as I flick through it. 'It's long for a poem but I'll read it aloud for you in sections.'

Coleridge is staring at me intently. 'When you do, you will appreciate the music, the soundscape of the natural world, the force of the metre.'

Now I understand. Coleridge has thought deeply about this present. He offered it to Grandma because she is the elder and head of the household but really it's for me, to read aloud. He picked up that I love poetry at Ama's when we were discussing the first note.

'OK,' I say, and when he looks puzzled, 'thank you!'

Big Ben is frowning. 'Are you Samuel Coleridge-Taylor or Samuel Taylor Coleridge? Tell me again.'

Big Ben takes longer to process the order of words, especially because he's heard of the poet.

'The former,' replies Coleridge, 'though I am partial to the narrative poem and would very much like to meet my late 18th-century namesake. His 'Kubla Khan' is an exquisite work. However, *The Song of Hiawatha* is my favourite. One day, I intend to write a musical composition of it.'

'Who are your father and your mother?' asks Grandma.

'My father is a doctor from the Sierra Leone Colony and Protectorate in West Africa. He left England to return there before I was born. I don't know him.' He pauses. 'My mother is a white Englishwoman from an extended family of musicians.'

Grandma does big-eyes at me.

'Elle, where are your manners? Serve the food!'

Dinner goes well. Coleridge especially enjoys the jellof rice and is fascinated with my colour-coolers. He says he wishes he had the equivalent to dampen sound – he's so sensitive to it. It helps with musical composition but is sometimes over-whelming in everyday life. He asks Grandma about Nigerian culture: what it was like growing up in the village and, of course, what music people danced to. For the first time, I hear her speak of the djembe and talking drum. Coleridge attends the Royal College of Music in London. He knows a lot about Western European music but not West African. He lights up when Grandma talks about the celebrations they used to have in the village.

After dinner, Grandma is tired and goes back to bed. As soon as she leaves the room Coleridge looks at the ground, but I know he's going to say something.

'Have you identified the writer of the note?'

'No. Did you know there's been a second one?'

Coleridge nods. 'Kwesi and MC^2 have made me an honorary Infinite since the Beat Battle. They informed me of your trip to 1888. I am based in 1891. Let me help you.'

'Do you have any ideas?' says Big Ben.

'I do,' replies Coleridge. 'I think the notes were composed by the same person.'

'What is your evidence?'

'They have the same style. They both begin with an imperative, a command: "Make me midnight!" "Search my area!" There is a similar punctuation of sound to . . .' He pauses. 'But I could be wrong . . .'

I look at Coleridge. That's his lack of confidence speaking. He's noticed something that could be very useful.

'Coleridge,' I say, 'similar to what?'

Coleridge looks down at the floor, embarrassed, but I can tell he's pleased. It seems to give him confidence to say more.

'To the composition at the Beat Battle. "Call me Sonos. Call me Chronos."'

'Which was written by Destiny!' I say. 'Do you think she wrote the notes?'

Coleridge frowns. 'It is possible. But I understand she is clever and new to the criminal gang. I do not believe she would take such an extravagant risk. And yet—'

'Who do you suspect then?' asks Big Ben.

Coleridge goes very still like he's concentrating. 'I do not like to make a judgement without sufficient evidence.'

'That's OK,' I reply. 'But I'm glad you reminded me of the

Beat Battle. I LOVED the music you composed for MC² and Kwesi!'

'Thank you, Elle. I wish to visit West Africa and the American continent to learn more about what MC² would call Black culture. But in the meantime, I welcome the chance to travel through time instead. And I would be happy to assist if you visit the Victorian era again.'

'Has MC² given you a Chronophone? We'll text you when we need you.'

I smile. For Coleridge, time travel is second best. But for Leaplings it comes first. We have The Gift to travel anywhere in space too but the thrill is in cutting through years, decades and centuries in a matter of minutes. I text MC². I've enjoyed this evening but I'm tired now. It's been a busy week; Big Ben and I have school in the morning. I hope it will be a gentle day but I have the strange feeling it won't be.

Chapter 11:00

DESTINY

Friday morning always starts with double PPF. This morning, I can tell Mrs C Eckler is flustered because there are strands coming out of the intricately coiled bun on top of her head. As we're taking our seats, Mr Carter enters the room with a tall man with light-brown skin and a long narrow face, wearing a dark blue suit. He offers the man a seat at the front of the room, then departs. I frown at the man; he reminds me of someone. Mrs C Eckler smiles at the stranger.

'Good morning, Tenth Year! I know you were expecting to continue with our Multiple Futures module today. However, this morning we have an unexpected guest instead. Please wear your name badges to help him.'

She pauses as we search our bags for our name badges and pin them on. She looks at me and I nod. Mrs C Eckler is very sensitive to my needs. She knows I need time to process and the few seconds we take with our badges is helpful. I'm getting better at coping with changes in plan but I still find it challenging. Once we are still, she continues.

'Today we are privileged to have Mr E, Director General of the Bissextile Investigation Division. Do not be alarmed; none of you are in trouble. But he is hoping you might be able to help him solve a case.'

As Mrs C Eckler sits down, Mr E stands up to face us all.

'Thank you, Mrs C Eckler.' He has a singsong voice but I can't make out his accent. 'To get straight to the point, I'm here on serious business. Our Leapling community is under threat: someone intends to reveal our secret time-travelling superpower, The Gift, to the media. We MUST prevent this serious crime before it happens.'

There's a group gasp as we take this all in. Our classmates are shocked at the thought of someone breaking the Oath of Secrecy; they're hearing this for the first time. But four of us are shocked because we're hearing this for the SECOND time. I try not to look at Big Ben, Jake and Maria but our eyes probably give us away. It's not only The Grandfather and The Infinites who know about the notes. The Bissextile Investigation Division know too. I wonder how they know.

Mr E is still speaking but I'm not listening to his tuneful voice. I'm looking at his face. I was originally distracted by his unexpected visit but now I know who he is. I've seen the same face at a different angle, in different circumstances. It's the face I saw sideways-on the first time I infiltrated The Vicious Circle in disguise. Then, he was number Four; now, he's Five. Mr E is not really Director General of the Bissextile Investigation Division at all: he's a member of The Vicious Circle!

If my eyes were wide before, they're even wider now. I can't say anything to my friends; I can't even text them. We're not allowed to use any kind of phone during a lesson. All I can do is take deep, slow breaths and try to pick up as many clues as possible about what's really going on. I tune in again to Mr E's voice.

'. . . suddenly leaping on their own, being more secretive. If you have seen anything unusual, speak to me in private after this lesson.' He pauses. 'Any questions?'

'Mr E, what does the E stand for?' asks Jake.

'That's for you to work out.' He smiles.

'What clues have you got?' Jake again.

I admire his cheek. Mr E is being direct with us so why not be direct with him? Mr E smiles with his mouth but not his eyes.

'We are not allowed to disclose evidence,' he says, 'but trust me, this threat is real.'

I raise my hand. 'Do you have any suspects?'

He looks at me for a few seconds as if he's not sure how to answer.

'Yes. We have several. But we need to narrow it down. If you've noticed anyone in your close circle, Leapling or Annual, acting strangely, I need to know. It might be something small or trivial but it could be a lead.' A strange beeping sound comes from his briefcase. He takes out a jet-black Chronophone.

'Speaking . . . Understood.' He turns to Mrs C Eckler. 'An important call. It will take some time but I'll be back in the second period.' He leaves the room.

'So, Tenth Year,' says Mrs C Eckler. 'The life of a crime fighter is very unpredictable. As Mr E is busy, we will continue with our Multiple Futures module for the rest of period one.' She pauses to turn on the giant monitor and give me and the class time to adjust. I'm thankful. Two changes of plan in ten minutes is very challenging for me. Mrs C Eckler continues, 'I'd like to show you a video of a show many of you will be familiar with. You will also be familiar with the star guest.'

The screen lights up with the first image, a circle with twelve symbols around it and it spins until one of them lights up: Pisces. Big Ben and I look at each other quickly then look back at the screen. The camera zooms into the Pisces symbol of two rotating fish which slowly becomes the face of a very old and horribly familiar woman with short white spiky hair: Millennia! Finally, the word *DESTINY* is emblazoned across the screen, there's audience applause and Destiny herself appears from behind glass panels at the back of the studio looking a little larger than in life, her mousy hair gleaming under the bright lighting, her bulbous brown eyes ablaze.

'Good evening, everyone, and welcome to the 2022 Halloween special of *DESTINY*, the only show in the world that accurately predicts the future. Tonight, we have in the studio a very distinguished guest who has come to ask me a very important question. But before she does so, let me introduce her: Millennia, welcome to *DESTINY*!'

Again, there's lots of audience applause as Millennia appears from behind the glass panel wearing a flowing purple trouser suit with a white blouse. She inches forwards gracefully with the aid of a stick and takes her place in the vacant chair to the right of Destiny, who joins her in the other chair.

Destiny smiles warmly. 'First things first: you were born a Pisces, raised in London and became one of the first women entrepreneurs of your generation. You made your millions in business. And now, I understand, you've turned your energies to technology. Tell the audience a little about this.'

'Yes. I believe the future is in artificial intelligence, machine learning. Robots in particular. I would like to invest in technology but my business advisors insist I put my money into ecological projects.'

Millennia has immediately gone into loudspeaker mode and I'm surprised she seems a bit nervous. This is probably her first time on mainstream TV. Destiny is nodding at her encouragingly.

'Millennia, I'm in awe of your many accomplishments and I'm already getting a very strong sense of your long-term horoscope. Please ask your question.'

Millennia clears her throat. 'Destiny,' she says, quietly, as if no one else was there but them, 'where should I invest my money: in an emerald ecological future or a silver technological one?'

'Great question,' replies Destiny, then speaks directly to camera. 'This is one of the burning issues of our age: we worry about global warming, pollution of the land and seas, the extinction of thousands of species. We can only guess what the world will be like in 30, 40 or 50 years from now. At the same time, we love our technology: our computers, our smartphones. What if machines became intelligent enough to help us find a cure for cancer, a solution to world peace? How do we make big life decisions? Ladies and gentlemen, you know the answer to this: ask Destiny!

'All my short-term predictions have come to pass. All my long-term predictions WILL come to pass. Millennia, hold my right hand. That's right. I see the answer in my mind's eye.'

Destiny has closed her eyes and is rocking slightly in concentration. As I watch, I get the impression she's speaking from a script; that the whole thing is an act. But she does so with such sincerity that I believe SHE believes it's true. When she opens her eyes, a giant smile crosses her face.

'Millennia, I travelled to 2050 and I saw a world run by super intelligent robots while humans had time to do the things they love most with the people they love most. The air was clean, the seas had not risen an inch, there were no freak weather conditions, and bees were buzzing in the sunshine. Global warming is not the threat we think. Invest in robots, robots, robots!'

I shudder, remembering Destiny in 2050 complaining that the icebergs had melted and global warming had spoilt her view. No way will the future look idyllic if we don't invest in greener cleaner energy. Destiny is lying. But why? It must be to push Millennia's agenda; to get businesses to put money into AI rather than green businesses. That's despicable. Not that Artificial Intelligence is bad; much of it is amazing if put to good use, as Ama always tells us. It's just wrong to outright lie about the state of the planet.

The video stops and the class erupts into chatter. Mrs C Eckler is looking shocked even though she must have watched the video before showing it to us. She nods at someone behind the glass panel at the top of the classroom door. A second later, Mr E enters the room again and stands beside Mrs C Eckler. He must have been waiting until the video was over.

'Welcome back, Mr E. We're just going to have a quick discussion about an episode of DESTINY. Then you can pick up where you left off. Are you familiar with the show?'

'I am indeed,' replies Mr E and I shudder. He's not just familiar with the programme, he knows the host and the guest too. 'I caught the last few minutes of this extract. I saw the whole episode live last week. Would it help if I joined the discussion?'

'Certainly,' says Mrs C Eckler. 'Now, Tenth Year, I know you are understandably upset about Destiny's disregard for the planet. And I know many of you are familiar with her programme. I must say, I was a fan until I saw it. But this module aims to look at an infinite number of futures and some possibilities will be controversial.' She pauses. 'Any questions? Yes, Maria.'

'We went on a school trip to 2048 hosted by Millennia and there was DEFINITELY global warming. There's global warming now in 2022. Why did she lie? And why didn't Millennia correct her?'

'A very good question, Maria. We Leaplings all know Destiny is lying and Millennia complicit in her silence. Innocent Annuals may believe Destiny's untruth, and who knows; the future may look worse than it does already. But remember, it could also be better if we radically alter the way we live. The future is not fixed; it is constantly evolving.'

Big Ben raises his hand and Mrs C Eckler nods at him.

'How many Annuals watch *DESTINY*?'

'I think I can help out on this one,' says Mr E. 'An excellent question. You want to judge the impact she's having. The figures range from an average weekly viewing of 10 million in the UK to 32 million worldwide. Of course, those figures do not differentiate between Annuals and Leaplings but you appreciate that Leaplings with The Gift are a serious minority. *DESTINY* is a very popular programme.'

'Any more questions, Tenth Year?' asks Mrs C Eckler. No one puts their hand up or speaks. 'OK. We have 20 minutes before breaktime and this has been an intense session. Remember, Mr E is keen to speak to any of you who might know something, however insignificant it may seem, about this threat to our Leapling community. If you have nothing to share with him, I'm giving you permission to have an early extended break. Don't forget about the 2050 work experience meeting this lunchtime. Those of you who wish to speak with Mr E, please stay behind.'

The room immediately clears of everyone except me and Big Ben, though Jake and Maria hover around for a few seconds to gesture they'll meet us outside afterwards. Mrs C Eckler looks intently at us as if to ask whether we want privacy and we nod. She leaves us in her classroom.

As soon as she's gone, Mr E transforms into Five. He seems to grow even taller, furrows his brow and his features become more chiselled and threatening. If I were a criminal, I'd be terrified of him. Then I remind myself, HE is a criminal. No wonder he's scary. Even his voice is less singsong.

'Glad you stayed behind of your own accord, Elle and Big Ben,' he says with a sneer. 'Did your social conscience get the better of you?'

'What do you mean?' I say.

'Don't play the innocent,' he snaps. 'You're too clever for that. I know everything you know and more; I've been around a bit longer. I appreciate you are wise beyond your years. A genius maybe, but still a teen. The Grandfather made a mistake employing you to solve the crime. A word of advice: leave this for the professionals.'

'You're not really an investigator, you're a gang member!' I say. 'Why should we take orders from you?'

'Actually, I'm both,' he says, looking so proud of himself that I know he's not lying. 'Another fact you are unaware of. The Vicious Circle are bankrolling the Leapling police force. Without us, they wouldn't exist. They do exactly what we say. So back off now, you don't know what you're dealing with.'

'We DO know,' says Big Ben, 'and we're not scared. We can solve the crime.'

'Finding lost kids and a museum relic is not the same as preventing a global catastrophe. Do you grasp the seriousness of this? The life of every single Leapling would be hell on earth. We'd be exploited beyond measure. We're dealing with a mastermind here; someone who will stop at nothing to gain power.'

That sounds like Millennia but of course it can't be her writing and sending the notes. I wonder if The Grandfather has confided in her. And I wonder what Mr E thinks of her.

'How do you know?' I say.

He gives me a hard stare. 'I know The Vicious Circle,' he replies. 'And so do you. Anyone who threatens The Vicious Circle feels no fear.'

'We didn't ask to take this on,' I say, 'but now we have, we're not going to stop.'

'Oh, but you are,' says Mr E aka Five. 'Because I'm telling you to stop. Begin by handing over the notes.'

'I don't have to!'

'You do. If you refuse, you will be arrested for withholding vital clues. It's a criminal offence.'

Big Ben nods. 'He's right, Elle. If you have the notes, hand them over now. If you don't, you should leap and get them.'

I frown at Big Ben. Why's he giving in so easily? Then I work it out: Big Ben is thinking that if we get arrested, we definitely won't be able to solve the crime. We can't give up now. I look at Mr E, who has a nasty smile on his face, knowing I have little choice. I'm sure he'd resort to physical violence; he looks like he could take on the two of us single-handed. We could leap away but then it would turn into a chase. It isn't worth it. I have the notes memorised perfectly in my head, down to the typeface of each individual word. And we don't have to have the original; it's not like we have the equipment to check for fingerprints.

I rummage in my bag and hand over the two envelopes containing the notes. Mr E puts on some white gloves and puts them into a clear bag which he seals. It dawns on me that my and Big Ben's fingerprints are all over both envelopes. Too late now.

We leave the room first. Jake and Maria are standing outside, like they were listening through the walls. Even though it's cold, we all walk out onto the school fields for some privacy.

'We had to give him the notes,' I say.

'You're joking!' says Jake. 'But it IS the police, I guess. Maybe they'll do a better job than us.'

'We're doing OK,' I say, though I wish we had more idea of who in The Vicious Circle was guilty. Maybe it's Mr E aka Five.

'Don't worry,' says Big Ben. 'I got photos of both notes on my Chronophone.'

'Good work!' I smile.

'You know that Halloween *DESTINY* episode?' says Jake. 'Should have been called Horrorscope!'

We all laugh. It's a bad joke but we need cheering up. I hear a car pull up very quietly in the staff car park. A silver Porsche! Mr E walks across the field and gets in. I squint to see who's at the wheel. Portia! For a split second she looks at us. Since The Infinites' last meeting, she hasn't responded to any of our texts. Either she was offended we considered her as a suspect and/or she's guilty of writing the notes.

Just before she starts the engine, Portia runs her fingers through her hair so it goes more spiky. It's a habit she has, but this time, it's like her hand is an afro comb and after each movement, it freezes mid-air. Big Ben and I exchange a glance. Oh my Chrono! That's an amber alert. Portia wants us to know she's

OK but it's too dangerous for her to contact The Infinites. So THAT'S why she's been avoiding us. I wonder what has happened. Portia accelerates out of the car park onto the school drive and shortly afterwards we see her Porsche take off into the sky and disappear into space–time.

I'm glad of the fresh air. As Mrs C Eckler said, it's been an intense morning. And not all bad: we've solved the mystery of Portia's silence since our brainbuzz, if not her strange silence during it, and we have more information for our mission. We might not have worked out who wrote the notes but we do know this: The Vicious Circle are gaining power. They run the Leapling police force and have power in the mainstream media. Destiny's a liar, a brilliant liar who likes being in the limelight. And she's publicly set on helping Millennia gain power.

Chapter 12:00

HIVES, HONEY AND HEXAGONS

What's the point in doing work experience when we're working on the most important mission of our lives? No wonder Big Ben and I neglected to organise a placement like the rest of the class. Mrs C Eckler offered to organise a morning at the Music, Maths and Movement School which would have worked well with our specialist subjects: my athletics and Big Ben's maths.

But then Maria stepped in: she reminded us that she and Jake were going to E-College-E in 2050 next Wednesday morning and there were still free places. Did we fancy it? We said yes because we knew Otto would be running a workshop and we might find out some useful information about him that could help in our mission. Also, we're both passionate about saving the planet. E-College-E is the ideal place to learn new eco practices.

It's now Wednesday the 9th of November 2050. We leapt from the same date in 2022 to the woods beside E-College-E to protect our secret Gift. We've been briefed that if anyone asks which school we go to, we should say we're home-schooled to avoid any probing questions. E-College-E is a series of bright white, split-level, flat-roofed buildings covered in plants from all over the globe. Even some of the walls are sprouting grass! This is only our second time here. The first was Halloween night, so we only saw the disco hall, which is where we are told to assemble before the first workshop we've signed up for: Queen Bee or Key Workers? Inventing your own job.

It's a bit chaotic in the hall because their Tenth Year pupils have organised the day. There are about 30 teens from E-College-E and 15 from other schools. I guess the host school want young people to learn management skills in a practical way. A few teachers are there to supervise though, and they introduce themselves informally. Mrs Storm is the first to come over. She's the teacher with purple hair we've met before on the Leap 2048 trip and seen onstage at the Beat Battle. She smiles with recognition.

'Hello Elle, Big Ben, Jake and Maria. Delighted you could make it, even though it was last minute for a couple of you.' She chuckles at her time-related joke. She knows all about Leaplings but is very discreet. 'I'll be running the first workshop. I'm really looking forward to your input.'

As she's talking, I notice another familiar face across the room, an old man with untidy white hair that looks like he's had an electric shock. His silver metallic jacket is a late '60s interpretation of the future. It's Otto, the judge who gave MC^2 and Kwesi a 6 at the Beat Battle, aka Eight in The Vicious Circle! He's talking to a small group of boys who are obviously mesmerised by him. But I'm not. I narrow my eyes at him; I'm looking forward to attending his workshop this morning. The more we find out about individual members of The Vicious Circle the better.

'If you'd like to follow me to the adjoining room,' continues Mrs Storm, 'we can begin our debate.'

I raise my eyebrows. I thought it was a workshop, not a debate. But maybe that's Mrs Storm's way of speaking. I soon discover it is. There are eight of us in this workshop, the four of us from Intercalary International and the other four from different local schools. We've barely sat down in the workshop room, shaped like a brain with grey walls that appear to be pulsating, when Mrs Storm begins.

'Welcome to Queen Bee or Key Workers? Inventing your own job. This is a practical workshop framed as a debate. I teach philosophy at E-College-E. I strongly believe that all ideas must be constantly challenged for the human race to progress. I do not believe in compromise; I believe if we extract the best ideas from diametrically opposed opposites, we find the best solutions.'

She asks us our names and allows us to divide ourselves into two groups. As we Intercalaries make no sign of moving away from each other, the rest of the teens shuffle into a unit and sit on the other side of the classroom.

'Good,' says Mrs Storm. 'Now, as you know, this establishment is called E-College-E for a reason. We must be in harmony with nature; if we are not, human beings will become extinct. And we can learn from other species. Some eat their own young – I wouldn't recommend that.' She smiles. 'But each lifeform has genius: ants understand collective power, rats are brilliant puzzle-solvers, bees create hexagonal living structures that show their mathematical creativity.'

Big Ben raises his hand. 'Hexagons are perfect because they use all the space with no gaps and are stronger than squares or triangles.'

'Excellent, Ben,' says Mrs Storm. 'But bees also have a hier-archical structure some would disagree with: the queen bee at the top, a few drones to fertilise the eggs, and thousands of worker bees below who do everything. The queen only has to lay eggs but she has to lay thousands of them; the worker bees do a broad range of jobs – nursing and caring for younger bees, building the hive, cleaning, maintaining or guarding the hive, making honey, attending to the queen, foraging for nectar and pollen to make royal jelly.

'Imagine the hive as a workplace: would you want to be a worker bee or a queen? Or would you restructure everything? That's what we're looking at today. Any questions?'

I raise my hand. 'So worker bees are like key workers – nurses and cleaners and builders?'

'Correct, Elle. Without them, bee society wouldn't function. And neither would ours. But without the queen bee, there wouldn't be any bees at all.'

Big Ben raises his hand. 'You said it's a debate. Do we have to write a speech?'

'Heavens, no!' says Mrs Storm. 'I'd like you to experience what it's like to be a worker bee. At the back of the room, you can help yourself to the virtual reality pads. Choose a job. I've tried it myself; it's an extraordinary experience!'

'Can I be the queen bee?' asks Maria.

'Unfortunately we haven't modelled the work of the queen or the drones. But there's a wide variety of worker bee jobs available.'

Maria swears in Portuguese under her breath but she soon brightens up. I dash over to the virtual reality pads. I usually hold back at workshops like this, taking time to process it all. But I've already decided what will be the most exciting job: forager. We learnt about bee roles in Sixth Year at my old school. Foragers get to fly outside the hive and collect pollen and nectar. When they do this, they help pollinate the flowers, which is essential for the reproduction of plants.

Big Ben is excited too. 'I want to eat honey and build hexagons!'

I tighten the helmet so it's firm but not uncomfortable and type the word 'forager'. It's like an immersive computer game. The numbers 3, 2 and 1 come onto the screen, then the job begins. It actually feels like flying at breakneck speed through a blur of countryside. It takes a few moments before I realise I can control it with my mind. Mind control again. Maybe that's what the future is all about: machines being able to mind-read.

I take deep slow breaths and it begins to slow down. I want to land on some lavender. I absolutely LOVE lavender. If I pass it overhanging the pavement outside someone's garden, I always rub my fingers against it then sniff them. The smell is just heavenly. I tried lavender honey once and found it too intense but I know bees love lavender.

A sea of purple comes into focus and the aroma makes me feel a bit dizzy. Curiously, my body feels itchy, like it's covered in dust. It must be the pollen in the air. I land on a lavender flower but before I can do anything else, I feel a sneeze coming on. It's one of those sneezes that takes a while to come out and I think I can stop it but I can't. ATISHOO! A massive explosion. Surely bees can't sneeze? I don't get hay fever but Big Ben suffers from it badly every summer. Now my eyes feel itchy. This is horrible. I take off the virtual reality helmet and Mrs Storm comes over.

'You're having a virtual allergic reaction, Elle,' she explains. 'It will only last a minute; it's not like a real one. You must have strong sensory sensitivities.'

'I'm autistic,' I say. 'My senses are heightened, especially smells. The lavender was too intense.'

'Here in the future, you might go for a job as a workplace consultant.'

'What's that?'

'Companies specifically employ neurodivergent people to enhance their workplaces. Autistic people notice flickering lighting, dust motes, lingering smells, substandard seating, environmental things that neurotypical people might be unaware of but affect us all. And some are also supersensitive to the mood of a workplace, how people work together, or don't. Dyslexic people are excellent at challenging our overdependence on the written word and those with ADHD have helped find new ways to help people focus on specific tasks.'

'So they value people who are different?'

'Yes! Society will never progress until it values those who think outside the box as well as those who think effectively inside it. That's why E-College-E partners with companies that employ a workforce with a range of neural pathways, lots of different ways of thinking.

'What job do you have in mind when you leave Intercalary International, Elle?'

'A detective.'

I'm surprised I said that. I was thinking professional athlete or writer, though I know they're not regular jobs you can apply for. But the word detective just came out.

'I imagine you'd make a very good one. The best detectives see things others don't.' She lowers her voice and adds, 'And I hear you and Ben did a great job on the 2048 school trip.'

I smile, remembering our first mission resulting in Big Ben and I becoming Infinites. It was only two years ago but it seems much longer.

'Thank you,' I say.

Mrs Storm addresses all eight of us.

'Please bring your virtual work experience to a close. Just THINK the word stop. OK, we're now going to see how you got on and whether you believe in a hierarchical workplace structure, one with a boss at the top and everyone working beneath them, or a level one, where no one is in charge and everyone is equally valued . . .'

I enjoy the discussion. Mrs Storm is delighted that we disagree but treat each other's views with respect. She says it is always important to listen closely to an opposing view. Maria unsurprisingly thinks the queen bee is the most important member of the hive and Big Ben thinks it's the builders. It's hard sometimes when you think BOTH people are correct. Sometimes there's more than one right answer.

The Infinites have a hierarchy: Kwesi is the founder member so the most respected; MC² and GMT are the next longest-serving members. All of them are Level 3 Infinites. Big Ben and I are Level 2. It seems totally fair, as they have the most experience. But when it comes to work, Big Ben and I do more than the others to get experience and improve our skills. They're brilliant at supporting us though. We both want to get promoted to Level 3 but only if we deserve it.

The Vicious Circle like their hierarchy too. A circle looks like a continuum, a shape with no beginning and end, but it's nothing of the sort. Destiny at One is poles apart from Millennia at Twelve. Millennia is queen bee; The Grandfather, her right-hand man; Meridian is a kind of Elder assistant; and everyone else is a worker bee. They each have different skills that help the evil gang operate.

In the bee hierarchy, there's only one queen. She stays queen until she dies and another queen takes over. If there's no one to take over, the whole hive can't operate. Someone in The Vicious Circle wants Millennia's job. Someone wants to be queen bee. The question is, who?

Chapter 13:00

OTTO'S MOTTO

The second workshop is on the other side of the school and is being led by Otto, number Eight of The Vicious Circle. Big Ben has been quite resistant to attending it because he suspects Otto of writing the notes. But Maria, Jake and I remind him how important it is to get evidence. Even more so if Otto is a prime suspect.

It's a small room, very different to a usual classroom with loads of quotations all over the walls and ceiling like 'It was the best of times; it was the worst of times' and 'It was a bright cold day in April, and the clocks were striking thirteen'. Only the four of us are attending this session. That's ideal; we can speak more freely amongst ourselves without having to conceal our Leapling status.

Otto seems to appear out of nowhere. One moment the four of us are chatting in a circle; the next, his voice interrupts our conversation.

'I am Otto,' he says. 'I'm Director of Studies here at

E-College-E. I teach English literature and drama. In this session, the enquiry is: What is Work? I'm asking you because I haven't the faintest idea.' He smiles but none of us smile back. 'A successful enquiry means questions. We can all ask whatever we want. We must not censor ourselves in the pursuit of knowledge.

'So who are you?' He peers at our name badges. 'Elle, Ben, Jake and Maria. I see. You are all from Intercalary International School.'

We don't say anything.

'Of course, you will not openly admit it. I respect you for keeping the Oath of Secrecy. But I am a Leapling too, so I make it my duty to know who's who. You were all clever enough to be chosen for that 2048 trip so you must be even cleverer now. And you,' looking directly at me, 'see yourself as a detective. So, here's a challenge: take this workshop. Teach us how to sleuth!'

I don't know what to make of Otto. He seems to be genuinely enjoying himself rather than being sarcastic. I want to dislike him because he marked my friends down and is number Eight of The Vicious Circle. But there's something refreshing about his unusual approach. He likes thinking outside the box.

He sits down with us, facing forwards. 'Go on, Elle. Stand at the front of the room, tell us about your work experience in the real world. Teach us something we can take away at the end of this session.' He pauses when he realises I'm not moving from my seat. I don't mind public speaking but no way am I going to talk about any of my missions in front of a member of The Vicious Circle. 'I see,' he continues. 'Can't teach or won't teach? That's the key to work. You have to have the knowledge and know-how to put that knowledge to good use for others.' He stands up.

'Now, you're all bright teenagers, which means you're cleverer than me. I might look like Einstein but I don't know an atom from a tomato. You can retain much more information than I can. You have access to more facts than I ever did which, if used wisely, you can build upon. But you don't know as much as me and you don't have much experience so you're going to have to respect me for the time being. Hahaha!

'So, you are here to learn about work?' Otto continues. 'Rule number 1: don't do it for the money; do it for the challenge. Rule number 2: make sure you're paid! Rule number 3: do something you're obsessed with. Rule number 4: don't let work take over your life. Yes. Work is a paradox. We love to hate it; we hate to love it. The poet Philip Larkin called work a toad squatting on his life but if I were a toad, I'd choose a better life to squat on. But Leaplings, if I may, what is work?'

'It's something you do for money,' says Jake without raising his hand as per usual. 'And you need money to live.'

'Not necessarily,' says Otto. 'You can be paid in potatoes or yams or free internet access or secret information. Or anything.'

Big Ben clears his throat and pauses before he speaks. 'You have to be able to measure it. You can measure it in time.'

'Very good,' says Otto. 'Time is the most convenient measure. We Leaplings know that. But you can also measure work in numbers, as in piecework, where you get paid per item rather than per hour. Alternatively, you might get a set fee for a big job like building a house.'

'If you measure it in numbers, you can give a mark out of 10.' Big Ben's still thinking about Otto marking MC² and Kwesi but applying it to the world of work.

Otto looks a bit flustered. 'We don't usually mark WORK out of 10.'

I raise my hand. 'You do if it's schoolwork. We get marks out of 10 all the time. And out of 20 and 50. It's easier for teachers to work a percentage out of 100 to measure how well we're doing.'

'Ah!' says Otto. 'But is schoolwork WORK?'

'It is,' says Jake, 'but we don't get paid. We should do. Then we'd have more incentive.'

'Schoolwork,' says Otto, 'should be for the love of acquiring knowledge, the love of learning. Every single subject is interesting if taught with creativity.'

'Why,' says Big Ben, 'did you give 6 out of 10?'

'Irrelevant!' says Otto and presses a button on his desk. A middle-aged white woman with a white straight bob appears out of thin air beside him.

'It IS relevant,' says Big Ben, ignoring the new arrival. 'MC² and Kwesi did lots of work on their rap. You gave them a 6 but they were the best.'

Otto puts on a theatrical voice and makes extravagant hand gestures.

'Intercalaries, meet Romana!

Teaches politics and drama.'

Portia told us Otto's wife is called Romana; this must be his wife, number Seven of The Vicious Circle. The white-bobbed woman gives a little bow.

110

'So you are the Intercalaries? I have been absolutely DYING to meet you all.'

'Why DID you give "Ghosts" a 6?' I ask Otto.

'It was not to my taste.'

'You gave "Bat Battle" a 10!'

'I LOVE bats,' replies Otto. 'I want to be a bat when I grow up. What do you want to be when you grow up?'

I can't believe he just said that. What a rubbish way of avoiding a question. Maria either falls for his act or she's trying another tactic. She's been unusually quiet by her standards.

'I want to be a professional high jumper,' she says.

'Of course,' says Romana. 'You're the one who jumps for Italy?'

'No, Brazil,' corrects Maria. 'But you and Otto are Italian? You have Italian names.' Some of Maria's extended family are Italian; she's spent some time there and speaks a little of the language.

'No, no. We are English but Otto and Romana sound much more romantic than Toto and, ahem, Gertrude.'

'My dear Romana,' says Otto, 'has been Juliet, Cleopatra and Pandora. She changes her name annually.'

'Is that to hide your real identity?' says Maria, looking innocent.

'I am an actress!' replies Romana without missing a beat. 'It is my job to conceal my true identity.'

'I thought you were a teacher,' says Jake. 'Or is that an act too?'

I'm shocked even Jake can be that rude but this is no normal workshop. Otto did encourage us to ask any question we wanted.

'What is work but an act between two points in time?' says Romana.

'What is life but a—'

Big Ben interrupts Otto. 'You tell us to ask questions but you don't answer them properly. That means you're lying. Why?'

'But I DO like bats.'

I raise my hand. 'Did you really give "Bat Battle" a 10 because you know Destiny?'

Otto says, 'No,'

and Romana says, 'Yes,'

at exactly the same time.

'Not logical,' says Big Ben. 'One of you is lying.'

Romana looks cross. 'Otto, tell them the truth. Destiny is exploiting your weakness.' She almost spits her name.

Otto looks as if he wants to crawl out of his own skin.

'If you insist.' He pauses. 'I gave Destiny top marks because I know and admire her literary skill. She is so talented I don't charge her but Romana doesn't believe in working for no money. You see, Destiny is my star pupil; I mentor her in poetry. Not at school – at, erm, work.'

He must mean The Vicious Circle but he can't say that out loud.

'So you helped her write "Bat Battle"?' I say, my mouth a capital O.

'Not exactly. I gave her feedback and tweaked a few lines.'

'That means you helped her. You should have declared your conflict of interest to the other judges. I'm going to tell the competition organisers.'

Otto smiles. 'I am the competition organiser.'

Big Ben frowns. 'Give the prize back. Now!'

Otto gestures to Romana and she grudgingly stands beside him. They hold hands.

'Well,' he says, 'as my esteemed mentor taught me: when you're cornered; leap forward!'

The two of them disappear into thin air!

I look at my friends. 'I can't believe they're in The Vicious Circle. They're not very brave.'

'No,' says Big Ben. 'They are cowards. And Otto is a liar.'

'A very bad one. I can't believe he virtually marked his own poem,' I reply.

'Maybe they don't need to be brave. Maybe they're rich?' suggests Maria. 'Or well connected. Or both.'

'They ARE rich. Portia said they've donated thousands to The Vicious Circle, remember. But they must be cleverer than they pretend,' I say. 'Doesn't Otto actually mean Eight in Italian?'

'Yes. But Romana doesn't mean Seven.'

'Elle,' says Big Ben, 'Otto spoke in rhyme.'

'Yes! Well, he does teach English and drama.' I pause as I realise what he's getting at. 'Maybe you've been right all along, BB. Maybe Otto wrote the notes. Now we've learnt he's mentoring Destiny in poetry writing, it would have been easy for him. But he's not the only rhymer; Destiny wrote most of the lyrics for Sonos and Chronos. MC^2 speaks in rhyme, but it's obviously not him. And lots of people are good at rhyme even if they don't show it. There are still lots of possible suspects.'

Big Ben nods. 'And Romana hates Destiny.'

'She hates Otto not charging her,' says Maria.

'Yes,' I reply, 'she said Destiny was exploiting Otto's weakness. But they don't exactly need the money.'

Maybe Romana is more angry because Otto showed favouritism by ensuring Destiny won the Beat Battle. Or maybe she's worried a strong character like Destiny might have power over a weak character like Otto in The Vicious Circle.

Chapter 14:00

MOI-MOI, CHIN-CHIN
AND PUFF-PUFF

'Elle, we need plenty flour, sugar and yeast,' says Grandma. It's Thursday the 10th of November after school. We're in the local supermarket and the trolley is overflowing with food and soft drinks. Usually on Thursdays I stay at school to do homework with Big Ben before he comes back for dinner but Grandma has insisted we go to the shops instead. Before we left the house, she said, 'Text your friend GT, Ama and Big Ben. Tell them to come at 6 o'clock.' But she didn't say why. I wonder what's going on. Maybe it has something to do with her leaping with The Grandfather.

As we turn down the baking aisle, Grandma puts four large bags of flour into the trolley.

'Grandma, why are we buying so much food? Is there a church celebration?'

Grandma smiles. 'Yes, there will be.' She pauses. 'Please, I beg, get three yeasts. I am too short.'

I always accompany Grandma to the shops as she can't manage on her own. Often her leg is paining her and she gets tired. But she refuses to let me go on my own; she likes to be in control.

'Now. Roasting chicken.' She counts on her fingers. 'Ten.'

'Ten? They won't have ten free range!'

'Free range too expensive.'

'Grandma, you know I feel strongly about this. When we eat meat, the animals must be reared humanely. Not factory farmed where they're fattened up in stinking sheds.'

Grandma sucks her teeth. 'Back home all our chicken free range. We don't make big profit.'

'I know, Grandma. That was different. Don't worry, I can leap to the farm shop and get some.' I pause. 'What else do we need? I might have to get a basket, we're running out of space.'

Guiding this overladen trolley round the supermarket is like circuit training. Thankfully late afternoon it's not too busy. We manage to get the last couple of free-range chickens and we join the short queue at the checkout. We always buy the meat last; Grandma has a thing about keeping it cool. I think that's from growing up in a hot climate without a fridge and things occasionally going off. She puts everything in the fridge she can possibly fit, even things that don't need it like dried apricots.

'Ah-ah! I forgot groundnut.'

That's what we call peanuts in Nigeria. We like to eat them roasted in their shells and the supermarket ones are the best. Before I can stop her, Grandma hobbles towards the snacks aisle. I feel a stab of compassion for her in my heart. She looks physically vulnerable and has been acting a bit strangely again today, more secretive than ever. I've invited my friends round but if there's a celebration, we won't have time to cook all this food.

Grandma returns with six large packets of peanuts just in time to add them to the bill. It comes to over £300 and I'm shocked it's so much money but I don't say anything. Grandma pays with her debit card and we leave the shop with the food bagged up in the trolley. We'll definitely have to get a cab. I'm so good at leaping now, I could just about manage to luggage Grandma and all the shopping but there's nowhere private enough to do so. Sometimes, not using The Gift is the better option.

∞

It's 5.45 and I'm sitting at the kitchen table with Grandma enjoying a cup of tea. We've put all the shopping away and yesterday's large pot of fish pepper soup is slowly warming up. The yam is boiling in a separate saucepan; we'll add it to the soup at the end. Grandma looks at me with her big bright eyes as if she can see right into my brain and read my thoughts. I feel a heavy feeling in my chest; Grandma's going to say something serious. She wants to tell me something important before my friends arrive.

'Elle, you are not yet a big woman but very strong. You have met the challenge of being autistic and used your poetic talent. You have faced your enemies and brought them to justice. Now you must face your greatest challenge: you must face grief.' She pauses and I hold my breath. 'Soon I will die. When I do, it will be very hard for you. But you have very good friends and a very

117

special Gift; you can leap through time. The Gift will enable you to see me alive again; the natural passing of the weeks, the months and the years will enable you to process your grief. Time will heal you.'

There's silence. I don't know what to say. Ever since Grandma leapt with The Grandfather then said, 'We all die. Death is part of life', I've known, deep down, that she'll soon die. But I haven't wanted to process it. Now I have no choice; Grandma has voiced it out loud and the shock of it floods my body with conflicting emotions. Sadness that imminently Grandma won't be alive in real time but excitement that as a Leapling with The Gift I'll be able to visit younger versions of her in the past. Fear that I'm only 14 and won't be able to cope with her death, but faith that I have good friends to support me who are like close family. I look at Grandma; she is being her absolute self in this moment, telling it as it is. It hurts so much but the hurt is charged with love.

I give Grandma a hug. She hugs me back. She always hugs hard and this one takes my breath away. After a few moments, she gently pushes me back, still holding onto my arms.

'Now. Your friends soon come. I will be very frank with them. Then we eat together. Now, turn off the soup.'

I nod and do as she says, draining the water from the yam, adding some to the soup but keeping some aside, in case GMT wants hers on a side plate with butter. Tears are welling up inside me but so deep down that it's going to take a while for them to surface. Grandma is my life; this will take some time to process.

'Grandma, when will you die?' My voice is a whisper.

118

'This coming Sunday. The 13th of November at 2.37 in the afternoon.'

In three days' time, Grandma is going to die. I still can't take it in. But I must because it's the truth. I take another deep breath.

'How do you know for sure?'

Grandma sighs. 'It is you who told me. When you are older, you visit me when I am younger. I demand to know; you tell me the exact date and time.'

∞

'You do not have to prepare the funeral; the church will manage it. I have already paid and they know all my wishes. But you must help Elle prepare the food. And GT, you understand the spirit. You will uplift Elle in her grief.'

Grandma is telling Big Ben, Ama and GMT how they need to support me in the next few weeks. Big Ben needs a few seconds to take it in, Ama's blinking away tears and GMT's taking notes on her Chronophone. I expected GMT to say something spiritual rather than be so organised but you can never totally predict how people will react in every situation. I think GMT will be very good at helping me cope emotionally in the next few weeks. Grandma has faith in her and so do I.

'Are you going to have a wake, Mrs Ifíè?' she asks.

'Not traditional wake,' replies Grandma. 'I don't want fuss. And I don't want long face. I have had a good life; I want you to celebrate it. After the funeral you must eat and do a dance for me. You must make party!'

'What food should we cook?' asks Big Ben.

'Chicken, fish pepper soup, jellof rice, moi-moi, chin-chin and puff-puff. Elle will give instruction; she is head chef!' Grandma looks at me proudly. 'I taught her well; now she can teach you.'

Big Ben frowns. 'What's chin-chin and puff-puff?'

'You had chin-chin here last Christmas,' I remind him. 'It's like fried biscuits. And puff-puff is Nigerian doughnuts. You'll love them!'

'Mrs Ifíè,' says Ama, 'Elle is very welcome to live with us in 2050 if she wants to. Mum's often said she sees you both as family. Or she could board at Intercalary and stay with us in the holidays.'

'Ama, I respect you,' says Grandma. 'I would like Elle to live with your family in the future. I have many times spoken with your mother and father. It is all arranged. Family is best.'

Ama looks at me and I know what she's thinking. It's not up to Grandma where I live; it's up to me. But I nod. Grandma's right. I don't want to be a boarder at our school and spend holidays at Ama's. I'd rather live at Ama's all the time. But I still want to go to Intercalary International so I can see Big Ben every day. I love attending the only Leapling school in the world and it would be good to keep in touch with real time, too. GMT makes a note of this on her Chronophone.

'What colour should we wear to your funeral, ma'am?' she asks.

'White or off-white,' smiles Grandma. 'And make sure Elle does not wear this her tracksuit. And that she wears good brassiere!'

120

We can't help laughing. Even when discussing her own funeral, Grandma can't help voicing her obsession. I ladle the pepper soup into bowls and serve everybody. We all sit down, Grandma at the head of the table. She says a prayer over the food and we eat. If I say so myself, it's fragrant, rich in flavour and the yam is smooth and firm; the best pepper soup I've ever made.

Chapter 15:00

THE THIRD NOTE

Today's Friday the 11th of November. I'm not going to school. How can I go to school when Grandma's going to die this Sunday? I can't think about anything else. Grandma informed Mrs C Eckler fully this morning, who insisted on speaking with me to check I was OK. She said, 'You can stay off school as long as you like, Elle. But equally, if you want the school routine, we are here for you.' That was compassionate of her.

I want to spend every minute I have with Grandma but she went straight back to bed, tired from her overnight cleaning job. I don't blame her. Even if you're going to die, you still need to sleep. Every hour I check up on her asleep in her bedroom. I don't often see her asleep; she looks peaceful. She says she used to check up on me every hour when I was a baby; now, it's the other way around.

She gets up at 4 o'clock in the afternoon, the time I usually get home from school, and we sit at the kitchen table.

'How was your day?' asks Grandma.

'Horrible,' I reply. 'I wanted to be with you and you were asleep.'

'Elle, you have plenty more time with Grandma on your time-line. Grandma can dance better than you when she was your age. Have faith.'

'I understand that, Grandma. But I already feel sad. And I'm scared of losing you. I can't imagine life without you.'

'Don't grieve me before I am dead, my dear.' She gives me a hug. 'You must stay strong; you have important work to do.'

'Grandma.' I pause. 'Why were you leaping with The Grandfather? I'm worried you're going to die because of him.'

Grandma shakes her head. 'It is not so. Do not be afraid of—' There's a loud knock on the flat door. 'Yes. It has happened.'

I frown. What does Grandma mean? We're not expecting anyone and I didn't hear knocking on the front door. Maybe it's one of the other tenants. I open the flat door and there's no one there. I'm about to close it when I notice something on the floor: a distinctive black envelope with a red seal. Another note!

'Elle, what is it?'

I come back into the flat and shut the door. I might as well share this with Grandma, though it's odd that she seemed to be expecting it. Maybe she can help decipher it.

'A note.' I put it on the kitchen table.

'Of course. The third note. Open it!'

'We opened the other ones tog—'

I stop myself. Should I tell Grandma about the other notes? But she must know already; she called this the third note. Grandma definitely knows more than she's telling me but I feel safe opening the note with her here. I can show the others later.

My fingers are shaking holding the envelope and Grandma gets a small knife from the drawers so that I don't rip it to pieces. The note inside is the same style as the previous two: a newspaper collage on white paper. This is what it says:

Anglesey? Early.
London? Late.
I'm from twenty past seven
to twenty to eight.

'Read it out loud!' orders Grandma and I do. 'What of the reservation?' she adds.

I check the envelope and notice a small, printed form that says Great Western Railway at the top. How could I not have seen it? It's handwritten in a scrawl quite difficult to read but I make an extra effort: the three-thirty locomotive from Paddington Station to Temple Meads Station, Bristol. November 11, 1844. Three passengers. Paid in full.

'We have to go on a train journey, Grandma.'

Usually this would be exciting but I'm finding it hard to rise to this challenge. I don't want to be anywhere else but the here and now. But Grandma has other ideas.

'Now. You must meet your friends in 2050, have a swim, then go on adventure. I will be here when you get back.'

I hesitate. 'Grandma, I can't concentrate on the mission because you're—'

'Yes, you can. I cannot tell you how but you overcome. With all your friends and that your poet from Sierra Leone.' She means Coleridge. 'There is much at stake.'

Grandma's certainly right about that. I feel emotional but remind myself that someone has threatened to tell the world about The Gift. I can't be selfish and give up on the mission. And it will help if I have something important to focus on rather than losing Grandma. I text The Infinites under Grandma's sharp gaze. Even tapping the keypad is an effort.

Emergency meeting at Ama's. 5 p.m. Note 3.

Then I hug Grandma tight, promising to be back a few minutes later in real time, and leap to Ama's front door, 5 p.m., Friday the 11th of November 2050.

∞

Ama's pool is in the only room in the house that's overground. The house is split level and the pool overlooks the countryside. It's an amazing view in summer but now it's pitch black outside. Ama soon remedies that: with a few clicks of a control, we have bright autumnal sunshine streaming through the glass.

'It'll make you feel a bit better, sis,' she says, squeezing my hand.

GMT agrees. 'And water's the best healer. Trust me.'

Kwesi signs, 'Water also helps the brain to flow. We gotta solve this riddle.'

All of us are in the pool, even Coleridge! Big Ben and I filled everyone in on the workshops in 2050, especially Otto's. Then I showed them the new note and reservation. I feel a bit guilty not inviting Jake and Maria to this meeting but I want a bit of privacy around Grandma's forthcoming death. We can tell them soon if we think it appropriate.

MC^2 does a whole length underwater. At first I think he's just showing off but he must have been thinking as well.

'Leaps, someone got an ego big as this house. They want us to catch them.'

Coleridge seems to be admiring the view but he unexpectedly speaks. 'Yes. They are giving a performance.'

'What do you mean?' I ask.

'They are composing the notes, imposing a setting. Each note is a development on the last.'

'Yes. It's like . . .' I say, trying to find the right words, 'a camera zooming in on something. The first note could have been anyone. The second one made it clear it was a member of The Vicious Circle. This third one is narrowing down the time. But it doesn't make sense. Why are they talking about Anglesey and London? Does that mean we have to travel from Wales to London on a train?'

Big Ben shakes his head. 'No. The reservations are from Paddington, which is in London. And the destination is Bristol, remember!'

At that moment, Robot enters the room with drinks and snacks. Big Ben can't resist.

'Robot, who wrote the note?'

Robot scans the note, as they did the first one.

'*The Times*, Wednesday, November 11, 1844.'

'Why does the note say Anglesey and London?'

'In 1844 there was a 20-minute time difference between Anglesey and London. The Great Western Railway used London time.'

'Of course!' I say. 'The first note was 1880 because that's when they standardised time. Before that, time was different depending where you lived in the UK.'

'So twenty past seven in Anglesey would be twenty to eight in London,' says Big Ben, floating on his back.

Ama takes a sip of her drink. 'But how does that fit with The Vicious Circle?'

'We must catch the specified train,' says Coleridge. 'I would be honoured to accompany you to 1844.'

'Is it very different to 1891?' I ask.

'From what I have studied, the trains are much noisier,' says Coleridge, wincing a little. 'And they lack heating and lighting. Whereas my commuter train is very comfortable.'

Coleridge commutes to the Royal College of Music every day so he's very used to late Victorian trains.

'I can come too if you like, honeybee,' says GMT.

She doesn't mean on the train; there are only three reservations. She means to give me moral support with all that's going on at home.

'I'll be OK,' I say. 'It will take my mind off things.'

The sensors on the ceiling glow a deeper blue, which means someone must have come through the front door. A minute later,

Ama's mum enters the pool space. She's a bit shorter than Ama, with her hair in long braids threaded with beautiful cowrie shells. A second later, her dad comes in too. He's tall and broad with short bushy ginger hair and heavy-rimmed glasses. He waves at us all.

'Looks like a full house. I'll have to design some extra rooms.'

'Anything you need?' asks Ama's mum.

'No, Mum. We're having a meeting.'

Mrs Atta Asante smiles. 'I wish my work meetings were like yours. Enjoy!' She looks like she's about to leave then says, 'And, Elle, remember you have always been welcome; you must treat this house as your home.'

'Thank you, Mrs Atta Asante,' I reply, feeling overwhelmed with conflicting emotions, moved by her kind words but devastated by the reason I'll soon be based in 2050.

As Ama's parents leave the room, I push off from the side and do a length of breaststroke, touch the side, flip over onto my back and swim back to my start point. My heart is thumping in my chest from my feelings and my exertion. Swimming helps my thoughts flow better, helps me see them with more clarity without consciously trying. My hair is soaked, which means my afro will be ruined; I'll have to spend some time washing and plaiting it so it's not an unmanageable frizz but I don't care. I feel a tiny bit better already. Water really can be a great healer.

When I swim, my mind is empty of worries. I focus totally on the element and enjoy how I breathe on every other stroke. It's a form of meditation very different to running. Running is about moving through the air. There's no resistance; you're aware of the outside temperature and your body getting hotter. And of course, as I'm an athlete, I'm conscious of time. My resting heartbeat is exactly the same as the second hand of a clock.

But I'm not thinking about that now. It's like the water has slowed time down, slowed everything down, even my thoughts. Then one thought comes into my mind and I let it in. We've just had the third note. What does it mean? We'll have to leap to 1844 to find out.

Chapter 16:00

RAILWAY TIME

Big Ben, Coleridge and I arrive at Paddington Station on the 11th of November 1844 in time for our train. Coleridge has lent us some Victorian clothes. They're old in his base year, 1891; a bit modern for 1844. But at least we're not wearing 21st century gear. We should blend in OK. Coleridge is in a black suit which looks timeless so he's inconspicuous apart from his untidy afro hair.

We leapt to a side street Coleridge said would be safe and luckily it was empty. I wasn't expecting it to be so cold; we could see our breath when we spoke and all around was deathly quiet. The station, in contrast, is busy and noisy. Above us, an elaborate glass ceiling; in front of us, all the trains are lined up and ready for action, glossy and black. Their funnels are like the top hats most of the men are wearing. Steam trains remind me of people who like to draw attention to themselves by huffing and puffing all the time. Some of them give off so much steam you can barely see them. The whole station stinks of coal and smoke.

To the far left of the station, in front of the trains, a crowd of people have assembled. Most of them look well off but one or two of the women are wearing faded brown clothes with thread-bare shawls around their shoulders. There's an elevated man in the middle, about 40, with wavy brown hair slicked to his head, giving a speech, waving his arms about dramatically. I assume he must be a preacher because he's dressed in black and is performing, almost singing, rhythmically like a list poem, but when we get closer, we realise he's listing all the things he hates about trains.

'. . . O spoiler of England's beauteous green pastures; O destroyer of marvellous vistas; O disturber of ancient monuments; O disrespecter of bird and beast; O stinking foul-breathed hell-hot monster; O generator of noise pollution; O multiplier of monetary greed: the devilish railway!'

We watch apart from the crowd as he finishes his rant and gets off his soapbox. People are asking him questions; he's clearly a bit of a celebrity. But Big Ben tugs at my arm.

'Elle, our train leaves at 3.30. We need to get on now.'

Once we've worked out which of the snorting steam trains is ours, and found our carriage, we step up into it from the outside. It's not like trains nowadays where you walk down an aisle. I shiver as I get on – as Coleridge warned us, clearly no heating in 1844 – but I soon forget about the cold. It's beautiful inside, all padded and ornate. The seats are velvet and even the ceiling is padded leather. It's not very eco-friendly but we are in Victorian times and this is definitely First Class. There are six seats in our carriage and only three of us so we spread out a bit. I like to sit facing the direction of travel by the window; Big Ben sits next to me. Coleridge takes the middle seat opposite Big Ben. The train noisily lets off a burst of steam; a whistle blows.

I check my Chronophone. 'I wonder if it will leave exactly on—'

'As I live and breathe,' shouts a familiar voice, 'I almost lost the train!'

The man who was ranting about trains throws himself into our carriage with a small brown suitcase a millisecond before a uniformed guard closes the door behind him. The train huffs, puffs, jerks and jolts its way slowly out of the station. The man steadies himself and sits down opposite me and beside Coleridge, who moves one seat to the left.

'You can't lose the train,' says Big Ben. 'It's too big!'

The man looks at Big Ben, amazed.

'Young man,' he says, 'it is, I believe, the current expression. My pocket watch says twenty minutes past three but that is Bristol time. Bristol is ten minutes behind London. But if I consult Bradshaw's Railway Companion, I am baffled,' he sinks into his seat, 'because I have the 1860 edition. The problem is, the timetable changes too fast and over 40 years. It is impossible to keep up. But keep up I must.'

I can't believe what he just said about 1860. It's 1844; only a Leapling would know what the future of the railway holds. And the only Leapling I can think of who knows a lot about trains is The Trainspotter. Surely it can't be? I look at the man. Either he's very good at acting or he's genuinely concerned and confused about the train times and doesn't care that he's given away his Leapling status. Does he know who we are? He doesn't seem very scary; there's three of us and only one of him. Since he's so open, I risk asking a question.

'Why do you hate trains?'

His eyes open wide. 'Who said I hate trains? I LOVE trains. But I hate the railway.'

'Not logical,' says Big Ben. 'Trains are made to move not stand still. You can't have one without the other.'

'Like time,' replies The Trainspotter. 'Time refuses to stand still. But I intend to conquer it. Know thine enemy!' I jump, hearing Grandma's words on his lips. 'You need to know your enemy inside out and back to front in order to conquer him. That is why I ride trains in my leisure time and am learning Bradshaw's Time Tables by perusing every Bradshaw's Railway Companion from 1839 until the 1880 Time Act. Once I know the exact second of every train departure in the country, I will have done my job!'

Big Ben smiles. 'Do you know the timetables for trains after 1880?'

'No, I do not!' replies The Trainspotter, spluttering his words. 'In 1880, they tried to fix time; but they failed. You cannot tell the sun when to rise and set! As for the 20th century, the railways scarred the landscape beyond recognition.'

Coleridge clears his throat. 'Sir, the railways have their use. They carry thousands of people to their study or employment.'

'And modern trains are good,' I say. 'The best ones are electric so they don't pollute the air like steam did.'

'21st century trains are the best! More eco-friendly than cars,' adds Big Ben.

If it wasn't obvious before that we are Leaplings, we've definitely given ourselves away now. The train jostles and The Trainspotter almost falls onto the spare seat. I try not to smile. Time to get back on track. I raise my voice over the sound of the steam.

'Do you have another job?'

'Yes. I sit on a committee investigating time travel. I take minutes for their meetings.'

Oh my Chrono; he must mean The Vicious Circle! But he speaks about them as if they're an ordinary employer. Maybe he's so obsessed with time, he turns a blind eye to working with an evil gang.

'Do they pay you?' asks Big Ben.

'Handsomely,' says The Trainspotter.

'You hate trains. What about cars?' asks Big Ben, before I can stop him. I was hoping to see what else he'd say about our enemies. Now we might annoy him. Cars weren't invented until the late 19th century and he seems to prefer everything before 1880. But The Trainspotter acts as if this is the most normal question in the world.

'The car is a work of art until it moves. As for the motorway, an abomination!'

He's starting to sound like a preacher again. I remind myself that we're on a mission; we're not in the same carriage as The Trainspotter by coincidence. Someone's arranged it; maybe The Trainspotter himself. Is he really as innocent as he makes out?

Coleridge looks down at the floor like he does before he speaks.

'Where are you travelling to, sir?' he asks.

'Llanfairpwllgwyngyllgogerychwyrndrobwllllantysiliogogo goch,' replies The Trainspotter, 'via Bristol Temple Meads. It is a village on Anglesey in North Wales. But I can't get there until 1869 when it acquires its long name. I am still devising my route through time!'

I widen my eyes, not at the long name which I love because it's a whole sentence bunched up into one word like German and the longest place name in Europe, but at the fact it's on Anglesey and 'Anglesey? Early' is the first part of the third clue. Well done, Coleridge, for asking that question.

'Anglesey is 20 minutes behind London,' says Big Ben.

'It is now. But to complicate matters, the Chester and Holyhead Railway will in future take their time from a signal gun in Llandudno which is sixteen and a half minutes later than London. They will only standardise in 1848.' He pauses. 'It is delightful speaking with you but I must now peruse current events and plan my next excursion.'

The Trainspotter unbuckles and opens his suitcase, takes out a large newspaper and begins to read. It's *The Times*! I look at Big Ben. Robot has confirmed that each mysterious note has been cut out and collaged from *The Times*. It may be a coincidence but he IS a member of The Vicious Circle so is already a suspect. Either someone wants us to THINK The Trainspotter is guilty or he actually is.

We eventually arrive at Bristol Temple Meads Station and leave the train.

'Well,' I say, 'The Trainspotter fits note number 3.'

'Yes,' replies Big Ben, 'but it was too perfect.'

'You don't think he wrote the notes?'

'No. Too obvious!'

'I agree with Big Ben,' says Coleridge. 'For a different reason. This gentleman could neither have the inclination to write the notes nor become the gang leader. It is not in his character.' He pauses. 'Do you wish to see the Corn Exchange where merchants conduct business? Its clock is famous for showing two different times: Bristol Time and Railway Time. But I forget, we are in 1844 not 1891, where I am based. The clock will currently only show local time.'

But Big Ben is looking at a different clock, the one at the front of the station and muttering under his breath.

'I'm from twenty past seven to twenty to eight.'

He closes his eyes for half a minute then opens them.

'Got it!' he says. 'It's not time, it's PEOPLE. Twenty past seven, the minute hand is pointing to the 4; twenty to eight, it's pointing to the 8. The writer of the notes is Four, Five, Six, Seven or Eight of The Vicious Circle. We've just seen Six but it's not him. That leaves four possibilities.'

'BB, you're a genius!' I say. 'What do you think, Coleridge?'

'I think,' says Coleridge, 'that Big Ben's deduction is correct. Now we must find more evidence.'

Big Ben has narrowed down the prime suspect to Chronos, Mr E, Romana or Otto. But we shouldn't leave out The Trainspotter. Surely he can't be as innocent as he makes out. And he's number Six of The Vicious Circle, exactly in the middle of Four and Eight.

Chapter 17:00

A TIME TO DIE

Today is Sunday the 13th of November 2022. Grandma is going to die at 2.37 p.m. I'm making her favourite breakfast, akara and agege bread, and all The Infinites except Portia have crammed into our tiny flat. Portia hasn't spoken to us since we brainbuzzed the prime suspect at Ama's house; and we haven't seen her since she gave us the amber alert when she picked up Mr E after he visited our school.

Everyone's hungry but thankfully they just want toast so it's not too much work for me. GMT and Big Ben have a great system going, cutting the bread and putting it under the grill since we don't own a pop-up toaster. Once we've all sat down – me, Grandma, Big Ben and GMT at the table; MC^2, Kwesi and Ama on the sofa – Grandma says grace. She finishes unexpectedly, addressing all of us.

'Now I have blessed the food, I bless you, friends of Elle. My name is Blessing Ifiè. I cannot read and write but after this day, that name will be written on document and tombstone. However,

I have had the privilege of travelling the timeline, the past and the future. You are Leaplings: you have conquered time. This will not be the last time you encounter me. So please, I beg, no long face. Eat your toast!'

Everyone smiles, including me, as they dive into the huge pile of toast, some of them choosing the hottest because they like the butter to melt into it. Grandma has always been direct and that is what I need right now, the truth and the motivation to get on with the everyday things in life. Like eating breakfast. I don't have an appetite but I make myself eat a little of the akara with Grandma because it's the last time we can before she dies. It may not be the very last time I eat with her. Maybe we do this again together some time in the past or in the future. Grandma will have already done it but I haven't done it yet.

I haven't asked her how many times I will see her after her death, or the dates and times. I like to know what's going to happen but not down to the last detail. I know how my mind works: it would become an obsession; I would not be able to function before each meeting; it would ruin my life. Whereas now I'm experiencing the mixed emotions only Leaplings with The Gift can have: the heaviness of grief in advance of losing my beloved grandma but the lightness of joy at the prospect of meeting her again in my life.

Big Ben stands up like he's going to make an important announcement. 'Who wants more toast?'

'Elle, where are your manners?' asks Grandma. 'Make the toast!'

But Big Ben and GMT have already taken over and Grandma admits defeat.

'You are blessed with very good friends. My funeral feast will be very sweet!'

'It will be an honour to cook it, ma'am,' says GMT.

'And eat it,' says Big Ben.

MC^2 is not to be outdone. 'I second that; minute it!'

GMT taps into her phone like she's really noting down what everyone's saying.

Kwesi signs in his own style, 'Madam, I'll do a special breakdance at the wake.'

I don't need to translate for Grandma; she's impressed with his moves.

'All of you will do a dance on me. Not just Kwesi.'

'Yes, ma'am,' smiles GMT.

Grandma smiles back. 'Now I must prepare for church. Elle, you will help me.'

∞

In her bedroom, Grandma sinks into her chair. I suddenly realise just how much of a show she has been putting on, making an effort for my friends. Now she looks even more exhausted than after leaping home with The Grandfather.

'Grandma . . .' I say, not sure how to continue.

'Elle, I tire!' says Grandma.

'I'll help you sort your handbag,' I say.

I do this as she ties her green headtie and a matching wrapper over her maroon leggings. I check she has her wallet and enough money for the collection, as I've done hundreds of times before but have never appreciated until now. Lastly, I put her gold Chronophone in. This prompts her to remind me, for the third time this morning, what should happen.

'When you get the phone call, come to the hospital by taxi with Big Ben, Ama and GT. Not by leap!'

'Can't I come to church with you? I might be able to—'

'No!'

The word falls like a stone. I've asked Grandma the same thing several times in the past two days and it's always the same answer. Previously, there was an explanation to follow. There's no need for one now; I know why. Grandma already knows how things will happen because some time in the future, I will go back in time and tell her.

I want to stop Grandma dying but I know it's impossible. And as if she can read my mind, she stands like she's making a speech.

'I do not fear death and you should not fear my death. The body die but the spirit survive. You will become a big woman and command respect. I am very proud of you. Before next week finish, you will see me again. What is the meaning of our name, Ifíè? Time.' She pauses. 'You have The Gift; put it to good use!'

We hug for five minutes but it feels like seconds.

Then Grandma stands, puts on her coat and I pass her the handbag. We both go into the sitting room where my friends are waiting.

'Good friends of Elle,' she says. 'Remember my instruction. Stay here and wait for the call. Now I am ready to go.'

∞

I'm in the hospital corridor with Big Ben, Ama and GMT near the room they put Grandma in. None of us are speaking but GMT has reminded me to do my mindfulness meditation to help me stay calm. Before the phone call, we went through Grandma's instructions step by step so we could all process what would happen together. In the taxi, I said a silent prayer for Grandma as she would have liked. It helped me too; I actually feel quite calm although my heartbeat is a bit faster than usual, like it is after jogging once round the track. It has also helped that the hospital has explained everything with compassion. Grandma has had a massive stroke. Would I like an end-of-life visit? I must not be alarmed that she will look different to usual.

Most of all, it has helped emotionally that Grandma has told me exactly what is going to happen next. The nurse will call me into the room; Grandma will not be able to speak or move but she will still be able to hear and understand everything I am saying. And I will say goodbye to her.

The clock on the wall says 2.25 p.m.; my Chronophone says the same. GMT squeezes my hand. I take a deep breath, hold it, then breathe out slowly to a count of ten. A middle-aged black nurse in a blue uniform appears from one of the rooms. She slows down as she approaches us.

'Which of you is Elle?' she says, looking at me and Ama. I like that she has a West African accent. The familiarity of it is like a firm hug.

I stand up. 'Can I see Grandma?'

I follow her into the room where Grandma is lying in bed

with lots of tubes coming out of her. There is a monitor showing what must be her heartbeat.

'You are brave, Elle,' says the nurse. 'Not all people can do this.' She peers at the monitor. 'Would you like a little privacy?'

I nod as I sit in the chair to the left of the bed and she closes the blue hospital curtains around me and Grandma.

'I must remain in the room since you are under 16 but please forget I am here unless you need me. This is your special time.'

'Thank you,' I reply.

Once the curtains are drawn, I am able to fully connect with Grandma. I reach over and squeeze her hand. She is not able to squeeze it back but I know that she feels it. I sense her response.

'Grandma,' I say, 'thank you for bringing me up.' I pause, not sure what else to say. You can't rehearse emotional moments like this; they just have to happen spontaneously. I feel an overwhelming flood of love and fear and sadness rising up from my belly before I add, 'And thank you for being you.'

I squeeze her hand again. No more words.

Grandma takes a very deep breath as if she's going to respond but I know she's not. I know she's taking her last breath. My hand is tingling as if her life force is flowing into me. It's the passing of the baton from one generation to the next; I have gained something but I'm not sure what it is. Strength? Wisdom? It is also the passing of time to the exact hour, minute, second of release. It is Grandma passing away. In that moment, I have a sense of physical loss, something else apart from Grandma.

It's 2.37 p.m.

Grandma is dead.

Sunday the 13th of November 2022.

For me, time itself stands still.

Chapter 18:00

THE TALKING DRUM

It's Friday the 18th of November already, five days after Grandma died. Today is her funeral. Her church bury congregation members soon after their deaths and believe relatives should grieve for a month. The community assist you in your time of need. Some of them have already visited the flat since her passing, bringing fried rice, chicken and soft drinks. Grandma warned me this would happen so I prepared what I would say to them.

I've had this week off school for compassionate reasons and Big Ben has also been granted the time off to support me. I don't know how to process the grief. We thought running would help me feel better but it's like my body's full of lead and my mind is too full of emotion for the emotion to shift. Mindfulness helps me focus on and accept my feelings for short periods of time but I also need a holiday from my own head. I've stayed at home watching Bob Beamon's phenomenal 1968 long jump world record on my phone. When things are difficult, that's the thing that makes me feel OK.

But something else is helping me. This morning I got a card in the post from Portia with a picture of a bee on it. Inside it said, 'Thinking of you' in gold letters and she'd scribbled a note underneath: 'Your gran was kind to me when I was missing Mum. She told me Mum wants me to live life to the full, not act like I'm still in prison like her. She cheered me up.' That made me smile. Portia only met Grandma once but once you meet Grandma you never forget her. It's good to have special memories of Grandma written down, even though they make me sad and happy at the same time.

I haven't been left on my own this week; GMT moved into the flat to support me because she's 18 but wise beyond her years so Grandma appointed her my guardian before I move into Ama's house. There has always been at least one of The Infinites with me, day and night. And I also have a Leapling social worker called Mrs Obeng who visits every day to check I'm OK, is sorting out all Grandma's paperwork and will be helping me transition to Ama's in 2050. Grandma appointed her too, with the help of Mrs C Eckler. I guess when you know your death date it's easier to be organised.

I thought I would become tongue-tied immediately after Grandma died but I'm not. I wrote a poem the next day and feel confident I'll be able to read it out loud today during the funeral service. I think I'm having a delayed reaction to grief. I haven't cried at all, though I feel as if the tears are deep inside me, like a well. That may be because I know I will see Grandma again and also because I'm autistic and might be processing grief differently to what I've read in books. I sometimes have a time-lag

145

between something major happening and my emotional response, like when the Infinity-Glass was stolen and it felt like everything was happening behind a glass screen. That said, everyone processes grief in their own way, there's no right and wrong. All I know is this: time is the best healer.

∞

The wake is being held in the church hall, which is a large room with eggshell-blue walls and a serving hatch at the back that opens out from the kitchen. It's even busier than the funeral – Grandma was very popular. I'm very moved that so many people have come to celebrate. Several of the teachers from my school have turned up to pay their respects, including Mrs C Eckler, Mrs Grayling and my athletics coach, Mr Branch. Most people are wearing lighter colours rather than black for their formal dress out of respect to Grandma and her church.

All of my friends attended the funeral, including Coleridge, and now we're sitting near the food hatch nodding our heads to the highlife music coming from the loudspeakers, apart from Ama, who is on social duty, making sure all the guests are OK. Highlife is popular jazzy West African dance music from the '60s that Grandma liked. MC^2 is swaying gently to the beat but his shoulders are a bit hunched; I can tell he's got something on his mind.

'So when's it etiquette to check out the dancefloor?' he asks. 'Me an' Kwesi need to get warmed up.'

'Warmed up for what?' I say.

'Dance for Grandma.'

One of the church members calls out from the kitchen and GMT and Big Ben jump to attention. It's their job to help serve the food. I join them there. With all these people, the music and my mixed emotions, I need some downtime. This is a comforting space, much smaller and smelling of Nigerian party food: tomato, chilli and sizzling groundnut oil. The saucepans are big as buckets yet somehow familiar. I remember church parties where I always stayed in the kitchen and read a book. I'm vaguely aware of the Pastor's wife asking GMT, 'Who prepared the rice, it is very fine!' and her and Big Ben bumping fists. They must be proud. It's the first time they've ever made it. I try a little on a plate and although I don't have much appetite, I'd definitely give them 10 out of 10.

Now, I tap my phone and watch Bob Beamon's long jump world record over and over again. The run-up, the leap, the kangaroo-hopping afterwards. Watching this usually gives me so much pleasure, I'm close to tears of joy. The others are in the main room, serving the elders. But here, in virtual privacy, watching my favourite visual of all time, I can't cry. It's not like I'm deliberately holding back; the tears just don't come.

The music has stopped in the main hall. I look through the hatch. Most people are sat at the side of the room eating the feast. Some of the male elders of the church are sat in a semicircle with djembe drums. As they begin playing, I find myself moving into the main hall, mesmerised, as if the drums are talking directly to my heartbeat. Some male church members and several women I've never seen before have formed a procession. The front man is wearing a black bowler hat and has a walking stick. The men behind him are wearing plain white tunics with traditional full-length gold and green wrappers underneath like Grandma used to wear; the women have elaborate Nigerian blouses and skirts in the same material as the wrappers and are holding plain white handkerchiefs which they jerk from side to side as they drop from the waist, rolling their shoulders in time with the drumbeats. It's traditional Izon dancing! Grandma loves, I mean, loved it.

Then the drumbeat suddenly changes, the beat simplifies and someone begins chanting over it in Izon. The voice reminds me of Grandma when she sang my name, 'Elle Bíbi-Imbelé!', and my heart floods with warmth and love. How can this be? But of course it isn't Grandma; it isn't even a person, it's a drum. I've heard of talking drums before but I didn't think they'd sound like real speech. And you'll never guess who's playing it with a curved stick? Coleridge! He really HAS immersed himself in West African music.

The procession disappears into the corridor and Kwesi and MC[2] appear almost out of nowhere, dressed in vests and shorts made of the same green and gold fabric. They bow to me before they begin so I know this is the dance in honour of Grandma. Their dancing is a mixture of the previous traditional dance and moves of their own. It's like the talking drum is giving them instructions for Nigerian breakdancing. They spin, they jump into the air, they zip across the floor at breakneck speed, their eyes wide with concentration. The drums become louder, more and more frenetic and the audience clap in time to the beat until they make an abrupt stop.

148

Everyone applauds, even the more conservative church members. The dance was outstanding and Coleridge's skills on the talking drum were almost supernatural. No wonder MC^2 calls him music maestro. It's only when I go up to thank them that I realise something has shifted in me. Music has reached into my heart; music is another way to help me heal. Thanks to The Infinites, this is a lively party, with great food, amazing music and very special dancing, a full celebration of Grandma's life.

But I'm not myself. I still have a long way to go; grief can do unexpected things to people. I'm an athlete, I know my body well, but nothing could have prepared me for this physical reaction that began the moment Grandma died.

At the end of the wake, we Infinites leave the hall with Coleridge and form a Chrono in the dark. We focus on my flat, real time, and close our eyes. But nothing happens, apart from a slight fizziness in the hands. Then we try again, this time with me in the middle with Ama and Coleridge, but nothing happens at all.

'Leaps,' said MC^2, 'this ain't gonna work. Elle's beat. We'll get the bus.'

But I don't think it's just tiredness; it's like I'm coated with Anti-Leap and that's thwarting everyone else's power. We're so skilled and are now so advanced, we can easily cope with a few Annuals. I didn't know it was possible for one person to have such a negative effect.

I can speak but I can't leap!

'It'll come back in time, honeybee,' says GMT.

But sometimes GMT can be over-optimistic. She doesn't just see the glass half full rather than half empty; she goes a step further. She says, 'We should be thankful to have the glass at all!' She's right but I can't imagine life without The Gift. What if I've lost it for good? It's not so much about having the skill, like being good at athletics, it's how I use it. How will I be able to fight crime on the timeline if I can't leap; can't be luggaged; can't be me?

Chapter 19:00

PORTIA'S PORSCHE

We're back at the flat. I'm so relieved to be able to relax in my own space with my friends. I'll be moving to Ama's soon; I want to savour the space I shared with Grandma as much as I can. GMT makes me a big cup of tea with two sugars; Big Ben puts on some ambient music, which is very calming. I love my friends but they can't replace Grandma. And the intensity of the funeral and wake has properly caught up with me. I need some serious downtime.

'I'm going to lie down in the bedroom,' I say.

'Who's staying over tonight?' asks Ama.

'Me and Big Ben,' replies GMT. 'You guys go get some sleep. It's been a long day.'

A few moments later, the flat goes quiet. I shut the door, knowing my friends are there in the sitting room if I need them. I lie down on the pink shiny cover of Grandma's bed. I've slept here every night since she died. I thought it would feel strange, since I've always slept on the sofa ever since we first moved here.

But I've found it comforting being amongst Grandma's belong-ings, smelling her hair pomade on the pillow. I can't bring myself to wash the bedclothes yet. I want to hold onto her warm scent as long as possible. How am I feeling? Empty, not just emotion-ally but physically as well. The emptiness is the loss of Grandma and the lack of The Gift. But I'm weirdly feeling full at the same time. Full of memories: immediate ones from the funeral and the wake but also lots of recollections of Grandma, things she said or did. I'm trying to be in the present like GMT says but my mind keeps flashing back to the past.

All my energy is spent on remembering.

∞

I'm five years old, sitting on the swing at the local park. I've been crying because my body feels fizzy so Grandma has brought me here before school. She knows I love the swings; they help me to calm down when I'm upset and not able to explain why in words. Grandma makes sure I'm secure then pushes my seat from behind.

'1 . . . 2 . . . 3 . . .' I count, with each forward movement.

She gradually pushes harder and I help by stretching my legs out in front of me before tucking in my lower legs with the backward motion. It feels wonderful, like flying! The roundabout always makes me sick but the swing is my favourite.

'. . . 57 . . . 58 . . . 59 . . .'

I'm aware Grandma isn't pushing so hard but it doesn't matter now. I've found my rhythm, I'm in the zone. I won't get into running till years later but it's a similar sensation: every fibre of my body revels in the regularity of the movement. It feels effortless. All my anxiety melts away.

'. . . 98 . . . 99 . . . 100.'

I stop counting. I stop my leg motion but the swing continues with the momentum. I wait until it stops and get off on my own. Grandma is sitting on the playpark bench. I'm not sure exactly when she stopped pushing me. She looks tired and her eyes are wet with tears.

'Grandma, why are you sad?' I say.

'I am not sad. I am happy! I did not know you knew how to count.'

∞

I'm 2-leap. Grandma and I are in a strange round dark room with no windows that smells like the woods after it's rained. I've been back to this room since; it's The Vicious Circle headquarters but back then it was used by The Oath Keepers. There are lots of people holding hands in a circle. Grandma and I swear the Oath of Secrecy together, repeating phrases after a disembodied male voice:

'We promise never to reveal to an individual . . . that Elle Bíbi-Imbelé Ifíè . . . is in possession of The Gift . . . unless under exceptional circumstances . . . Furthermore, never to reveal The Gift to the masses . . . or face a prison sentence from 20 years to ad infinitum.'

Sensory overload kicks in and only snatches of conversation

break through, like '. . . Gift is extraordinary', '. . . met her older version?', 'Fight against the evil . . .'

∞

I don't usually play this whole memory back but now Grandma is dead, I want to know everything about her. I now understand what older version must mean: Grandma promised me we'd have some great times ahead. She's already met the older version of me. Maybe she met my older version before I was even born! That must have been odd.

Why are these particular memories haunting me? They both remind me of The Gift, The Gift I've lost. And of Grandma. Grandma took me to the swings before she made the connection that the fizziness in my limbs related to The Gift rather than a sensory sensitivity from being autistic. Grandma took me to The Oath Keepers once my spectacular Gift was confirmed.

Now I've lost my Gift and The Oath Keepers are The Vicious Circle. Surely new Leaplings don't go to The Vicious Circle to swear the Oath? But they wouldn't be any wiser. They would simply swear the Oath of Secrecy and leave. They wouldn't know how evil for power The Vicious Circle are; that Millennia wants to control people's minds through technology. Or that someone is threatening to reveal The Gift to the masses, the mass media, unless they are made the new leader of The Vicious Circle!

The thought hits me again: how can I discover the writer of the notes if I can't leap or be luggaged? Then another thought that's been niggling me ever since Grandma died: she seemed to deteriorate after she leapt with The Grandfather on the night of Halloween. Grandma never explained what happened that night. Maybe the mystery of the notes and Grandma leaping with The Grandfather are connected.

'I need to see Grandma to find out!'

I realise I've unintentionally spoken the second bit out loud and GMT knocks on the door.

'Elle, did you call?'

'No. But come in.'

She opens the door and sits down on Grandma's chair. 'Should Big Ben come in too?'

'Yes.'

Big Ben enters the room and sits cross-legged on the floor on the other side of the bed. I sit up on the bed, my back resting against the pink quilted headrest.

'How can I see Grandma if I can't leap?'

'Elle, do you think you're ready?' says GMT. 'She's only been dead five days.'

'I'm ready,' I say. 'She said "Before next week finish, you will see me again."'

'That gives us two more days,' says GMT, looking thoughtful. 'A word of advice, Elle. When you DO get to see Grandma, be careful what you say about her death. Folks freak out when things get outta synch.'

'That's already happened,' I say. 'Grandma knew she was going to die years before she did. She was acting oddly the whole week before. I think it was hard for her knowing the date but not wanting it to be true. She got a bit confused.'

Big Ben closes his eyes, deep in thought. I hope he has a good idea; I'm counting on his logic. A minute later, he opens his eyes.

'Portia's Porsche,' he says.

'Brilliant idea; cars have more leap power! But it may be tricky for Portia to help us,' I say. 'Remember her amber signal.'

'I'll steal it!' he says.

'BB, no!'

I'm remembering the first time, which was also the last time, Big Ben stole a car: Season's Ferrari Forever. He crashed it. I know his driving has improved since then but that's not a great track record. I get my Chronophone out of my bag.

'I'll text her,' I say. 'If she doesn't respond . . .'

'. . . she'll have to resign. Infinites stand together, not apart.'

I know Big Ben's being extra protective of me but that's not really fair on Portia. She could be in real danger by keeping in touch with us. Sending me a card is one thing; responding to a text is quite another. I tap into my phone.

I can't leap since Grandma died. Please drive me to visit her on Halloween.

I press send and lie back down onto the bed, exhausted from the emotional intensity. Almost immediately, my phone buzzes!

OK. Can I come now?

Oh my Chrono! I wasn't expecting such a quick response. I tell the others, though GMT insists on reading it aloud. She can't

156

quite believe it too. After a few moments, I text back and we all go into the sitting-room so we can look out of the window onto the road. Portia's most likely to leap to the industrial area then drive to the flat from there. It will only take a few minutes. Sure enough, five minutes later we see the silver Porsche parking opposite the flat.

'Shall we come too?' asks GMT. 'To support you.'

'OK,' I say. 'You two can stay in the car with Portia whilst I visit Grandma. Maybe Portia can explain why she's been avoiding our calls.'

A minute later we're in the car. Portia doesn't say anything until she's driven to the industrial area and stopped the car.

'I'm so so sorry I've been incommunicado,' she says. 'And for being so ratty during the brainbuzz. At first I was upset you thought I'd written the notes but that didn't last long. Things got extra tricky. I had to stay away from The Infinites. The Vicious Circle are tracking me. You know Destiny's teens were controlling my car. Now they're trying my phone! I got it protected but it's only a matter of time.'

'Does that mean they might have seen all our texts?' I say. 'They know you're a double agent!'

'Maybe,' she says and we all gasp. 'But I could always pretend I was investigating YOU!'

'They haven't threatened to exit you?' asks GMT.

'No,' says Portia. 'If they do know I've betrayed them, they're waiting for the right moment to confront me.'

'Why did you come now?' I ask.

'Because you've just lost your grandma and I want to support you. I was too scared to come to the funeral in case The Vicious Circle tracked me and turned up.' She pauses. 'But I don't think they'll arrive on your doorstep. You'll be safe on this trip. Trust me.' She starts pressing buttons. 'So what's the date, time and place?'

'Monday the 31st of October at 10 a.m. The morning of Halloween. Here is good, then we can drive back to the flat.'

Grandma leapt with The Grandfather that evening. I know there's no point in trying to leap after that point. Grandma's lips were sealed. But perhaps if I leap before that episode, she might be more open to telling me how she knows The Grandfather and whether she knows anything about the notes. Portia keys in the details, revs up the Porsche and soon we're leaping back in time effortlessly. Clever Big Ben. He always has a solution. Soon I might be one step nearer to solving the mystery, helping my friends and seeing my beloved grandma again.

Chapter 20:00

GRANDMA'S SECRET

My heart is thumping in my chest like I just ran the 100 metres as I unlock the door to our flat and step inside. The past week, I've felt grief in my heart as a physical pain but never fear. Now I'm nervous as well as distraught; hyperaware of every movement I make, every detail, like the lumps in the gloss paint of the kitchen window when they redecorated our entire living space. It's like entering the flat for the first time.

At first I think Grandma must be out because the kitchen is quiet. She often listens to gospel music on the radio but not today. Her bedroom door is open so she must be in there. Yes, she's sitting on her bed in front of the dressing-table mirror tying her blue-green zigzag headtie which matches her wrapper but clashes with the chunky purple cardigan she often wears once it gets cold.

Grandma hasn't heard me yet. I stare and stare like every extra second with Grandma is precious, is the last. She seems so real, so alive. She IS alive now; my head knows that. But my heart feels the absence. Now I'm here, I don't know what to say. I remember GMT's advice to be very sensitive with Grandma, to not reveal that she's going to die soon. Grandma finishes adjusting her headtie and turns to me slowly, like she didn't hear the key in the lock and assumed I was standing there staring at her all the time.

'Elle, make me a cup of tea. I slept late.'

I don't move. I can't move. I've never disobeyed Grandma before; that's how she brought me up. Respect your elders. I feel the deep ache in my chest move up to my throat and my eyes sting with tears. Then comes the avalanche of grief I couldn't let out at the funeral. I no longer feel human; strange, strangled noises are coming out of my mouth and I'm rocking backwards and forwards. But in the middle of this, I also feel relief.

Grandma stands up and the next thing I know, we're on the sofa in the sitting room. She's hugging me tight like she used to when I was a little girl and that's exactly how I feel: like a little girl too young to deal with this. Knowing Grandma has been dead for almost a week yet feeling her hugging me as if she's never going to let go is too much of a paradox. Maybe it was too early to leap back to see her after all. Maybe I should have allowed the grief to settle.

But I remind myself that the reason I've leapt back in time is to ask Grandma questions, help solve the mystery notes and bring down The Vicious Circle. And underneath all that, I must find out why Grandma was leaping with The Grandfather and whether we even SHOULD decode the notes. Maybe it's a trap and The Grandfather has written them himself.

160

Once I'm too exhausted to sob any longer and Grandma can see that I need a bit of space, she rises to fetch me a box of tissues and begins to make tea in the kitchen area. I already feel a bit better. There's something so solid, so no-nonsense about Grandma that grounds me. Always. This could be a regular day, except Grandma is making the tea and not me.

Grandma making tea in the kitchen is giving me more time to process what is happening here. As the kettle begins to boil, she puts the teabag in my favourite white mug with the fading gold rim and gets the tinned milk from the fridge. I see her adding three sugars, knowing that on this occasion I won't challenge her for being unhealthy. I think as I take tiny sips, for once in my life, too much sugar is good.

Now, Grandma sits back on the sofa and fixes me with her big, bright eyes and for a split second I see a softness I haven't seen since I was 2-leap.

'Elle Bíbi-Imbelé Ifíè, you know I love you more than myself. Like a daughter. Since I raise you, I know you are special. You have The Gift. This month you have been missing school and asking a lot of questions yet not remembering my reply on the same day. Yet you have good memory and I thought, "something is wrong somewhere". Now I know why; there are two of you this month: one in the present and one from the future. You are from the future today.'

I nod, blow my nose and take a gulp of the sweet tea. Grandma continues.

'I cannot read and write but I know how to reason. You cry tears of grief but I know your friends live long life. There is only

161

one possibility: it is me, Grandma, who is dead. Grandma will die soon.' She pauses, frowning, taking it all in. Just hearing her say it aloud, I feel the sobs begin again but she shakes her head.

'You told me the date and the time of my death many years ago but I chose not to believe it. Now I believe it. Elle, listen to me-o! No more tears. What is done will be done. You cannot prevent my death. If it has happened in real time, that is what will happen.'

She squeezes my hand hard and the warmth surges through me, as if she is giving me life itself. It reminds me how energised I feel just before leaping, like I've been supercharged. It also reminds me of the surge of power I felt from her the moment before she died. Some of her words surprise me: I never thought for a moment of going back in time to try to stop Grandma dying. Some Leaplings might desperately try to change the past but not me. I too accept her death is irreversible. But it reminds me that I chose to come back primarily not for myself but for The Infinites. Plenty of time in the future to leap back and spend quality time with Grandma. That's the advantage of being a Leapling with The Gift.

I open my mouth to speak and nothing comes out at first. But I persevere, knowing being with Grandma has already begun to . heal me. I know I haven't lost my voice this week and I'm not going to lose it now. There are things I must find out. I don't know how to do this, how to ask those questions that have been keeping me up at night for the past week. Grandma has seen me tongue-tied many times and knows all I need is time and space. But this is different. This is not knowing what to say. When I speak, my words sound hollow like the ghost of my voice.

'Grandma, do you know The Grandfather?'

Grandma sighs so deeply, she seems to shrink into the sofa. She looks at me with her big bright eyes.

'I knew one day you would ask. That day is today.' She pauses. 'What is the meaning of Izon? Truth. Today I must reveal to you the truth.

'I met The Grandfather when you were 2-leap and we swore the Oath of Secrecy. The Grandfather runs a service, he was very open about it; he helps old people leap across time and space. The demand is high in Leapling community. It is expensive but cheaper than airfare and much faster! He made good profit. He has been helping me for years.'

I look at Grandma and she looks a bit embarrassed, as if our roles have been reversed in a different way to the tea-making; I'm the responsible adult and she's the tearaway teen. Suddenly, Grandma being extra tired the past few years makes sense. It wasn't so much the multiple cleaning jobs; it was all the leaping. It takes it out of Annuals more than Leaplings. Though of course, Grandma has never revealed her true birthday. She may be a Leapling herself but age has made her too weak to leap alone.

'When and where did you go?'

'Nigeria.'

She only answered half my question. I frown at the thought of it.

'Why The Grandfather? He's a criminal! I don't like you leaping with him.'

As soon as I've said it, I realise how useless it is to complain. Nothing I say will alter what has already happened.

'*He that is without sin among you, let him first cast a stone.* The Grandfather is discreet, respects his elders and he learns the error of his ways. I work on his soul over time and he repents.'

I'm reminded of the older version of him trying to distance himself from the evil teen version. Maybe Grandma's right; maybe he's not 100% evil for his entire life. But then I'm reminded of something else.

'He . . .' I want to say that he leaps with Grandma later this evening and after that she is weak. I want to say that he might have indirectly killed her but I don't know what I'm allowed to say. As GMT said, it wouldn't be fair to tell Grandma what WILL happen on her timeline, especially as it's bad. She already knows she's going to die soon. I don't want her last days to be any worse.

'Elle, you are 14 years of age. You are young adult with good brain. It is time I tell you my secret. I leaped to Nigeria to see your father.' I widen my eyes with surprise and she pauses to allow me to process. 'Your father is not a good man. He abandoned you after your mother died and went back to Nigeria. He became kidnapper! He has been in prison in Nigeria for many years. But I did not abandon him. He is my son, my own flesh and blood.'

Hearing about my father is a shock but I don't feel an emotional attachment. I don't remember him at all. But I feel angry that Grandma has been putting her life at risk to see him. It's like she reads my mind.

'Love knows no fear. Leaping is cheaper than aeroplane and you return the same day.'

164

I smile in spite of my anger and finish my tea, which is now cold milky syrup at the bottom of the cup. Grandma has a point; leaping has definite advantages.

'That is better!' says Grandma, meaning my smile. 'Now we must take photograph on my Chronophone.'

'Why?'

'I like to keep track of us together. Today is a rite of passage for us both. You have gained knowledge; I have confessed.'

She gets up from the sofa with some difficulty, stiff from sitting for so long, goes into her bedroom and returns shortly with her gold Chronophone and a pink plastic carrier bag. She hands me her phone and I take the photo of the two of us. We're not smiling – it's too intense a moment for that – but there is love in that photo.

Grandma takes the phone off me and swipes with surprising dexterity considering she has rheumatoid arthritis in her hands as well as her knees and feet. I remember MC^2 being surprised Grandma had a Chronophone but it all makes sense now. That must be how she kept in touch with The Grandfather across time. Suddenly she looks up.

'This phone has recorded the past, the present and the future. When I'm gone, keep it safe until you are 5-leap. Then you can look. But in this moment in time, there is one photo I must show you.' She pauses. 'The best.'

I raise my eyebrows in expectation, wondering what it will be. She fumbles in the pink plastic bag and pulls out a large, framed photo. The colour has faded and it looks really retro. It's of two young black women with huge afros and identical bright orange shades, one much taller than the other. I frown at the shorter one. It's hard to see how old she is. Probably a mid-teen.

'Is that you, Grandma?' I guess and she nods. 'Who's the other woman?' I pause and she smiles. 'It's me, isn't it! You and me together. When was it taken?'

She takes the phone back from me and smiles with tears in her eyes.

'*The thing that hath been, it is that which shall be; and that which is done is that which shall be done.* Elle, I have known you all my threescore and ten. We have done many things together. Some of what has happened to me is yet to happen to you. I have lived my life; you are still living yours. When you are older and I am younger, we meet again several times in the past and in the future. You have much to look forward to.'

I give Grandma a big hug, making a mental note that three-score and ten means 70 years old. She softens a little, then gives me a look like she wants to say something important.

'Please, I beg. I hope you did not wear this your tracksuit to my funeral. And you wore good brassiere!'

'Grandma!'

It's like nothing has changed at all. And everything has changed. Grandma dying has turned my life upside down. Yet seeing her today, though the pain is still there and will take a long time to heal, I feel a bit more like my old self. Grandma is bustling around in the kitchen. Things are definitely normal again, if that's possible.

'Cook before you leave for your Halloween party. I intend to visit your father after work and will need to eat when I get back.'

She shakes her head. 'I am confused. You are future Elle; you have already cooked. Tonight will be the last time I see your father. I will say goodbye to him and remind him he has done one good thing in this world: produce a fine daughter.'

'Grandma, I'm not feeling fine at the moment. I'm too sad to help my friends. You told me to know thine enemy to defeat him but I don't even have the power to leap. It's too painful.'

'Time will heal. Today you found solution to leap here; next tomorrow you find your power.'

I take a deep breath. 'Grandma, I want to solve a mystery. Someone is writing wicked notes.'

'I know,' says Grandma. 'And I know who wrote them.' She pauses. 'But I will not disclose their identity to you. You must discover it yourself. You and Big Ben will solve the mystery. You do not yet know thine enemy but the day you do, all will be revealed. You will say one word and your adversaries will destroy one another!'

'What is the word?'

'The name of prime suspect. But they are innocent.'

'Thank you, Grandma,' I say, wishing she didn't speak in riddles but knowing she's never going to tell me directly. She and MC² have a lot in common.

Grandma frowns at me. 'How did you travel back? Did The Grandfather luggage you?'

'No, Grandma.' I shake my head vigorously. 'I came by car.'

'Have a good trip!' she says and gives me a hug. It's a short, firm hug that means not goodbye but *au revoir*: see you again.

Chapter 21:00

THE FINAL NOTE

The next morning it's Saturday and I've just changed into my tracksuit when I get a text from Portia. It's a group text to all The Infinites.

> Another note! Elle and Big Ben must go to Moon & Sons on 28 February 1900 at 11 p.m. I'll drive you.

∞

Portia's hair is extra spiky, which means she's anxious. She doesn't say it, but I guess she still suspects The Grandfather and thinks this is a trap. She must also be worried that he might have worked out she's a double agent and deliberately sent her to pick us up. I'm glad she stays quiet; my heart is already beating hard in my chest with the anticipation. I couldn't cope with more emotional overload.

Portia has to park the car somewhere discreet, even though it's an hour before midnight. She waits in the car whilst Big Ben and I walk to The Grandfather's shop.

'I'm glad Portia drove us, I still can't leap,' I say.

'Me neither,' says Big Ben.

'What do you mean, BB?'

'It's 1900. An anti-leap year. There's no 29th of February this year. Today is the 28th of February.'

He reminds me that century leap years have to divide by 400 not by four for the calendar to work across time. 1600 and 2000 were leap years but 1700, 1800 and 1900 were not. It's much much harder to leap to anti-leap years.

As we approach Moon & Sons the door opens abruptly and The Grandfather teen ushers us in.

'Fun and games,' he says and smiles his grimace smile. 'Another note.'

He hands us a familiar-looking black envelope with a red seal. I take it and put it carefully in my bag the same moment that his older self, The Grandfather 1900, appears from thin air in front of us. He's visibly aged from the last time we saw him in 1888. His hair is grey, white in places, but his face is etched with lines that look more from worry than from age.

'Leave my premises immediately,' he says, 'unless you have the skills of a trained midwife! My daughter, Rosalind, has begun her labour. We are about to become a grand—'

'Elle and Big Ben were just leaving,' interrupts The Grandfather teen. He turns to us. 'I'm counting on you to solve this. I want

169

all the proof and the name of the suspect: one word. And you got to be there in person to say it.'

∞

Portia drives us to Ama and Kwesi's in 2050 for an emergency morning meeting. We detour back to 1891 to collect Coleridge then stop off at 2022 to pick up Jake and Maria. They've all proved themselves during this mission and we need all the help we can get.

Ama's mum and dad welcome us all, then leave us to it in the games room. As soon as they shut the door, I get the note out of my bag and put it on the table.

'Open it,' signs Kwesi.

My fingers aren't working properly, I've noticed that too since Grandma died, so Big Ben helps me. My voice trembles when I read it out loud.

**Sounds like I'm one
of your Infinite friends.
I am a symbol
that never Ends . . .**

'Easy,' says Big Ben. 'Infinity!'

'No!' say GMT and MC² at exactly the same time.

Kwesi's shaking his head. Jake and Maria look shocked.

Infinity, our mysterious leader. Infinity who oversees The Infinites and decides when we level up. Surely Infinity wouldn't threaten to reveal The Gift to the media. And she certainly wouldn't want to run The Vicious Circle. Or would she?

'We can't think with our hearts; we have to think with our heads,' I say. 'Infinity DOES sound like the word Infinite. And Infinity is also a symbol that never ends.'

'Logical,' says Big Ben.

'So who out of Chronos, Mr E aka Five, The Trainspotter, Romana or Otto could be Infinity?'

MC^2 fills Jake and Maria in on how clue number three narrowed down the suspects and our Victorian train trip where we met The Trainspotter. Maria narrows her eyes.

'Infinity is a woman,' she says. 'So it must be Romana. She's an actress and changes her name every year.'

'She does,' I say, remembering her flamboyant personality. 'But we don't know for ABSOLUTE certain that Infinity's a woman. We mustn't rule out the others.'

I remind myself of the suspects: Chronos, the teen rapper; Mr E, head of the Bissextile Investigation Division; The Trainspotter who hates railways and told me 'Know thine enemy'; Romana and Otto, the husband-and-wife team who both work at E-College-E and are funding The Vicious Circle. None of them seem right.

Ama looks deep in thought. 'Could it be one of us?'

'What you sayin', sis?' asks MC^2.

'It says "Sounds like I'm one of your Infinite friends". This person could be someone outside The Vicious Circle who knows about The Infinites, which is worrying. I thought only Infinity knew we existed. Or it's one of us.'

Kwesi signs. 'But none of our names are "a symbol that never ends".'

I think of all our names then the ones that are most unusual. Ama and my name are palindromes, MC^2 is a formula, GMT is an acronym. Kwesi's right; none of them are a symbol.

Coleridge clears his throat. 'Elle, have you begun reading *The Song of Hiawatha*?'

'No,' I say, embarrassed he will think I didn't appreciate the gift. 'Grandma only died two weeks ago. I haven't felt much like reading yet.' I pause. Now it's Coleridge's turn to look embarrassed. Then he looks thoughtful.

'"He the best of all musicians, / he the sweetest of all singers . . ." These notes remind me of some of my favourite lines from the poem. Not the exact metre but there is always a strong stress at the beginning of the line. In all four notes.'

'Like Otto's Motto,' says Jake.

'What's that?' asks MC^2.

'"When you're cornered; leap forward." He said it before he disappeared.'

Portia snorts. 'Reminds me of something The Grandfather would say. I'm sure he's behind all this. What year were the notes linked to? 1880, 1888, 1844 and 1900. Who's based in the Victorian era? The Grandfather. Who delivered all these notes? The Grandfather.' She pauses. 'Don't look at me like that, Elle, I know The Grandfather better than you do. I have a weird feeling he's enjoying all this!'

'I agree he's enjoying being theatrical,' I reply, 'but it doesn't add up. If he wanted to run The Vicious Circle, he could easily oust Millennia; he's an Ancient. I don't know who to suspect.'

'Make me midnight; Search my area; Anglesey? Early; Sounds like I'm one . . .; When you're cornered.' Coleridge is creating a soundscape.

'Coleridge, do you think Otto wrote the notes?' I ask.

'It is the same style,' replies Coleridge. 'But as we said previously, anyone can imitate a style, especially if they are familiar with another's work.'

'Otto teaches English AND judged the Beat Battle,' says Jake. 'He could easily have written them.'

'And Otto's a palindrome,' says GMT, 'which means he'd fit with The Infinites. Two of us have palindrome names.'

'AND Otto means eight,' adds Maria.

Everyone looks at her.

'Oh my Chrono!' I say. 'The number 8 is an upright infinity symbol. "My name is a symbol that never ends." Infinity didn't write the notes; it was Otto!'

∞

Big Ben and I have retreated to the bottom of Ama's house to the snug, which is the smallest room but still the same size as Grandma's bedroom. It's much quieter here, easier to think. I appreciate the input from the other Infinites but sometimes it gets a bit much when everyone's coming up with ideas. I work much better 1-2-1 or on my own.

I must make notes about what I'm going to say to The Vicious Circle with Big Ben's input. If I don't write it down, I don't know how it will come out of my mouth. I won't be nervous but it will be very difficult not to insult them all. It's going to be a very strange experience, standing up in front of The Vicious Circle to denounce one of its members. But it has to be done.

We begin with the first clue, remembering how it was so general, it could have been anyone in the whole world, then noting how with each clue we narrowed down the suspects from 12 to five to one. One word: Otto. My head says it must be Otto but something's niggling at me. What is it?

'BB,' I say, 'I feel like we've got the answer but it's not the answer.'

He frowns. 'Not logical.'

'Sorry for talking in riddles. And I know it's not logical, but I feel as if there's more than one answer to this problem. It IS Otto but something doesn't quite fit. Something's wrong!'

'The clues are too easy,' says Big Ben.

'This one wasn't,' I say. 'You thought it was Infinity at first.'

'But we solved it quickly,' Big Ben persists. 'If you make the clues easy, you want someone to solve it.'

'What if we're supposed to think it's Otto but really it's not. What if it's someone trying to frame Otto?'

Something stirs in my mind. I close my eyes like Big Ben does when he's working out a maths problem. My leap visit to Grandma before she died. Our conversation about this mission. What was it she said?

'You will say one word and your adversaries will destroy one another!'

'What is the word?'

'The name of prime suspect. But they are innocent.'

I open my eyes with excitement. 'BB, what's likely to happen if we accuse Otto?'

Big Ben closes his eyes for a full minute. 'Otto is number Eight. If he goes, this happens: "When a member exits, the remaining members move clockwise to fill the spaces, unless they are under a reprimand or due a promotion."'

He's quoting Millennia's exact words when he and I witnessed a meeting hidden under the table on our last mission. He still has the audio on his Chronophone and I know he listens to it from time to time.

'So, everyone moves round until the number One chair becomes vacant,' I clarify. 'Or if Millennia wants to humiliate or reward someone, she can make some changes.'

'Correct,' says Big Ben.

I have an idea who really wrote those notes. I might be wrong but if I'm right, it will fulfil Grandma's statement. One word will bring down The Vicious Circle. I know Otto is innocent but I will publicly say he's guilty. I don't like to lie but this evil gang must be destroyed. In fact, it will self-destruct and accusing Otto is the only way to make it happen. I want to tell Big Ben my suspicion, but who knows if Ama's house has been bugged? I whisper it into his ear. His eyes widen. Now let's see if I'm right . . .

Chapter 22:00

THE ENEMY WITHIN

It's noon on Sunday the 20th of November 2022. Big Ben and I are standing in the circular oak-panelled headquarters of The Vicious Circle. The last time we were here we leapt secretly under the central round table to recover a stolen museum piece. This time we've been formally invited by The Grandfather. Thankfully, Portia didn't have to drive us here; that would have been too risky for her and us. MC² has been giving me some 1-2-1 mentoring and GMT's been meditating with me. My leaping powers have come back! Thank goodness they have; I was worried they might have gone for good.

All 12 members are present: all wearing their purple hooded cloaks except The Grandfather in a Victorian three-piece suit, all standing in a circle around the table. Millennia is at the head; the equivalent of number 12 of the clockface. Then going clockwise there's Destiny, Portia, Sonos, Chronos, Mr E, The Trainspotter, Romana, Otto, Nona, Meridian and The Grandfather. The middle people have their backs to us and their hoods up but I know who they are; Mr E couldn't resist giving me a long hard look when he appeared behind his seat.

The Grandfather puffs out his chest. 'You may be seated,' he says, but remains standing himself. Everyone obeys. Everyone except Millennia, who narrows her cat's eyes in our direction.

'In the name of Time, what are THEY doing here?'

'Elle and Big Ben have come to give evidence,' replies The Grandfather, 'for a crime against—'

'There has been no crime!' says Millennia.

'Agreed, esteemed leader. We're stopping the crime before it's been committed. But there's been a threat: a threat to The Vicious Circle and every Leapling with The Gift.'

'I was not informed of this, Grandfather. Why did you not follow the ancient protocol? And how can it be that our enemies are witnesses?' Millennia has gone into loudspeaker mode.

'Investigators, more like.' The Grandfather seems to be looking at Mr E, whose head twitches under his hood. Millennia winces. So The Grandfather informed Mr E about the notes but not Millennia. That's why Mr E knew so much when he visited our school. And now Millennia knows she's been kept out of the picture. That must sting. The Grandfather continues.

'Chrono of crime, thieves of time, let us commence!

'Now, we're all aware that our esteemed leader is Millennia. Some of us might think we could do a better job,' he grimace-smiles, 'but we respect her position. However, one of our circle wants the top job so bad, if we don't give it to them, they'll tell the world we can leap through time.' He pauses. 'Who is it? Elle can tell us.'

There are several kinds of silences. Some are hushed with awe, some are full of wonder; this silence is deathly. I look around the circle at the terrible 12. Correction, I face the evil 11. I remind myself that Portia is definitely on our side. She looks terrified, even more scared than when she was publicly arrested last year. The Evil Nine and Ten look angry, which is surprising since Big Ben and I have witnessed both Nona and Meridian showing their lack of respect for Millennia. Millennia herself is staring right at me. If looks could kill, I'd be dead.

I take a deep breath like I'm about to run the 100 metres sprint and begin.

'The Grandfather received four anonymous notes. He employed me and Big Ben to work out who wrote them. The first note was the threat he just mentioned. At first it could have been anybody but the second one gave us a clue that it was a member of The Vicious Circle.'

'Must we listen to this girl's false accusations?' asks Meridian in her gravelly voice.

'Hear her out,' says The Grandfather. 'Elle, continue.'

But I'm distracted by the interruption and Big Ben speaks instead.

'The clue was about the area of a circle: πr^2. It was someone in The Vicious Circle.'

Evil Nine snorts. 'Why would they draw attention to themselves? Did they demand money?'

'No!' The sharpness of my own voice surprises me. I dislike Evil Nine intensely. 'Some people want to be in the limelight. Or prove how clever they are.'

'And how clever are you, Elle? Do you think you could do MY job?' It's Mr E and his voice is more sinister than singsong.

'Silence!' says The Grandfather. 'Elle, tell us about the third clue.'

'It was a riddle based on the different times in the Victorian era. Before time was standardised.'

Big Ben smiles. 'I worked out it had to be members Four, Five, Six, Seven or Eight.'

I love that Big Ben is confident enough to stand up to The Vicious Circle. I was happy to speak on my own but his input is so helpful. It gives me time to process everything that's happening. I still can't quite believe we've been INVITED to The Vicious Circle.

'Nonsense!' shouts Mr E. 'That's what you get when you give teenagers power. They make stuff up.'

'I agree,' says Romana. 'They are so creative, their power exceeds even mine.'

'But then we got the final note,' I say, 'and narrowed it down to one.'

Silence.

I continue. 'The clue said, "My name is a symbol that never ends."'

'At first I thought it was Infinity,' says Big Ben, and one or two members jump at the name. 'But Elle worked it out.'

'With help,' I say.

The Grandfather can contain himself no longer. 'So who wrote the notes?'

I meaningful pause before I say the key word. 'Otto!'

179

Several things happen at the same time.

'Help me hence, ho!' says Romana and dramatically falls onto the floor.

Destiny smirks; Portia's mouth forms a capital O; and Mr E rapidly clicks his Chronophone.

Two giant hooded figures appear behind Otto.

Otto says, 'When you're cornered; leap forward!' and begins to disappear but is frozen in time, half here, half in the future, held in the vicelike grip of the two Bissextile Investigation Division robots. 'Or maybe not,' he mumbles. 'But I'm innocent. I've been framed!'

'Good work, Five,' says The Grandfather to Mr E. 'Nice to see your arresting officers are up to speed.'

The robots swiftly disappear, taking the outline of Otto with them. The Grandfather continues.

'And congratulations, Elle and Big Ben. You've done a good job. You should be proud of yourselves.'

I don't know whether The Grandfather is being sarcastic or not. I expect Millennia to say something negative but she totally ignores us. She always pretends to know nothing about the crimes committed by her gang or anyone else connected with them. That saves us; to her, we're now invisible. Millennia has stood up, imposing in spite of her advanced years.

'Well,' she says. 'Good riddance! We cannot tolerate threats or delusions of grandeur. I will miss the generous financial donations but I hope Seven will remain in The Vicious Circle and continue to support our enterprises.'

Seven, aka Romana, has sat back in her chair but looks very

shaken. I doubt she'll want to stay in The Vicious Circle now her husband's just been arrested. Millennia continues.

'Eight has been exited; there is therefore a vacant position. Under normal circumstances, I would follow protocol and suggest that One to Seven each move clockwise to fill the space. One would then be vacant due to rotation. However, one of our members has excelled themselves in recent weeks. Due to her lightning speed work recruiting technical teens and exceptional contribution to my media profile, I am promoting Destiny from One to Eight!'

For a split second a triumphant smile dominates Destiny's face. That gives her away. I don't think anyone else has noticed, apart from Big Ben, who knew my suspicion. Destiny used Otto to win the Beat Battle and wrote the notes in his style to frame him. Coleridge was on the right track from the very beginning. And as Maria said in our brainbuzz, Destiny's power crazy. She calculated that if she got rid of Otto, Millennia would promote her to fill his position. Now it has happened! Destiny gets up from her chair and begins to walk clockwise around the circle. But she doesn't get very far. Mr E has already stood up to block her.

'Not so quick, young lady! It takes years to advance to an Eight, not weeks.'

'Five, you have the audacity to challenge my authority?' says Millennia.

'I do, esteemed leader,' says Mr E.

'And so do I,' shrieks Romana, who has miraculously recovered from her fainting fit and no longer looks shaken, just angry.

'I would rather set fire to Eight's chair than have this girl sit on it!'

Destiny looks at Mr E and Romana and yawns. 'All my life older people have underestimated my skills. Only Millennia sees my true value.'

'Millennia is deluded,' says Nona and everyone gasps. 'If she insists on this promotion, she is not fit to be leader. It shows a complete lack of judgement. She has not even consulted with the Elders.'

All colour drains from Millennia's face. 'If I am hearing correctly, Five, Seven and Nine are opposing Destiny's advancement. Five and Seven might be forgiven for speaking out of turn. Five's position at the Bissextile Investigation Division has gone to his head but he remains useful; Seven is melodramatic as ever but remains rich. But you, Nine, have overstepped the mark. I have suspected your disloyalty for some time but now I have evidence.' She goes into loudspeaker mode. 'YOU are the enemy within. Nine, from this second forth, you are exited.'

'No one exits me!' says Evil Nine.

'I have just done so,' spits Millennia. 'You can no longer rely on your family name. Half of your relatives are rotting in Do-Time. And if you do not leave these premises within the next minute, I will have you forcibly removed so you may pay them a permanent visit.'

'Esteemed leader,' begins Meridian, 'You have not followed the correct—'

Millennia turns on her. 'You too undermine my authority? First Grandfather chooses not to inform me of a grave threat to my own position, to The Vicious Circle and every Leapling that has ever existed. Instead, he tells my ENEMIES. And now you, Meridian, attempt to discipline me.' She pauses dramatically. 'Five. Operation Zero!'

Five presses a button on his Chronophone and immediately the evil gang is surrounded by robots: The Circle is encircled!

'Now,' says Millennia, 'this is what will happen: Destiny will take her new seat; Nine will exit; and you,' looking at Meridian, 'will learn that Ten o'clock does not have the power of Midnight.'

'Esteemed leader,' replies Meridian, 'I do not desire your power; I see how it has corrupted you over time and it disgusts me. Therefore, from this moment forth, I exit The Vicious Circle.'

'I think not,' says Millennia. 'I am exiting YOU. To Do-Time. When I think of the crimes you have endorsed, it disgusts ME.'

Meridian is seized by the two robots standing behind her. She opens her mouth to protest but is luggaged immediately.

Evil Nine sneers. 'I am not intimidated by your methods. You will pay for this.'

'You have ten seconds,' says Millennia.

Big Ben and I watch open-mouthed as Evil Nine refuses to leave and she too is luggaged by robots.

Millennia turns to the one remaining Elder, the evil teen. 'Grandfather, founding Ancient, what happens next?'

The Grandfather shrugs his shoulders. 'I'm out! Fun and games are over. You got what you wanted, but at what cost? Nine and Ten can't be replaced; without the experience and the Elders, the Circle's finished. You can't recreate it with new Leaplings:

the young ain't got the wisdom and the old are old enough to know better. I'd arrest this group of losers if I were you, especially Destiny.' He pauses for effect. 'Yes, Destiny. She wrote the notes for promotion. Oh, she knew she'd only reach Eight today but there's always the future. You better watch out, Millennia, she wants the top job. She meant what she said: Make me Midnight! Now there's no Elders, she's got less competition.'

'Nonsense!' screams Millennia. 'Destiny is loyal. Who is spreading this wicked misinformation? Her?' She suddenly points at me and it's like I've been struck by lightning.

'Not Elle,' says The Grandfather. 'Elle did what she had to do. A little old lady warned me of Destiny before she died. Her son's inside for kidnapping; she knew a thing or two. Ever since I met her, she's been singing the same tune. "Boy," she would say, "you got two choices in life: good or evil." I've been evil up to now but you can have too much of a bad thing; now on, I'm batting for the opposite team.

'Goodbye, Granddaughter. And don't expect to be luggaged no more, I got a clockshop to run.'

He takes his hat off to me and Big Ben and disappears into thin air.

Millennia nods at Five and the robots disappear too. Destiny calmly sits in The Grandfather's vacant chair and Millennia does nothing to stop her. I can't believe her cheek. I'm dying to see what happens next but Big Ben and I hold hands and leap back to Ama's games room immediately in case Millennia turns on the Anti-Leap and we're trapped. A split second later we're joined by Portia. The Infinites surround us. Then it all hits me and I can't take anything else in, except that several Chronophones have been buzzing with good news. Coleridge has been promoted from honorary status to a Level 1 Infinite, and Big Ben and I have been promoted to Level 3! But more importantly, in spite of her evil intent, Destiny has helped The Infinites to destroy The Vicious Circle for good, with a little help from Grandma.

Chapter 23:00

ROOT FOR THE FUTURE

It's winter solstice, the shortest day, Wednesday the 21st of December 2022. We've chosen this special day for our levelling up ceremony. Now that I have formally grieved Grandma for a month and have my leaping skills back in full force, it feels right to celebrate our victory over The Vicious Circle.

I'm now living at Ama and Kwesi's house in 2050. I'm still getting used to the unpredictable weather outdoors and the massive space indoors. The house has huge rooms so I spend much of my time in the snug, which is more like our old flat, small and a bit run-down, even after the decorating. But I'm not in the snug now, I'm in the lounge, a huge white square room bordered with gold vegan leather sofas and multiple bean bags. I prefer the bean bags.

You need eight people for the ceremony to make the infinity sign so we have the perfect number in order of rank: Kwesi, MC^2, GMT, me, Big Ben, Ama, Portia and Coleridge. I'm so pleased Coleridge is being promoted because he helped so much during our mission analysing the poetry. He worked out those notes were written by Destiny ages before anyone else did. And he also supported us on the Victorian train trip. The brilliant water drum background music playing now is his latest composition. I remember him on the talking drum and I smile. Coleridge is helping me grieve Grandma too.

It doesn't take long before Robot has joined the party and we're ready to begin the ceremony. I always get butterflies before an initiation, it feels so special. This task has been particularly difficult because Grandma died. But I've been brilliantly supported by my friends. I make a mental note to thank Jake and Maria for their input too when we go back to school in January.

'Choose an initial or the initial will choose you!' Kwesi signs and MC² translates for Coleridge.

'I would like to be C,' says Coleridge, 'for it is not only my initial but C major is the first musical scale I learnt on the piano as a child.'

'Good choice,' says MC². 'The letter ain't already taken. It's yours, bro!'

Then the eight of us assemble into a loose circle. I get a horrible flashback to The Vicious Circle but we hold hands and snake into a large infinity symbol. That's better! We have to stay silent for a minute according to tradition. After that, Kwesi, the most senior member, draws an imaginary infinity symbol onto Coleridge's hands.

'Coleridge is now an Initiate, a Level 1 Infinite,' says MC², 'same as Ama and Portia.'

Then Kwesi does the same to me and Big Ben.

'Elle and Big Ben are now Level 3 Infinites,' continues MC^2, 'like me, Kwesi an' GMT. Congrats all! You ready for that tattoo yet, Elle?'

Only MC^2 can get away with this teasing. He knows I would never get a tattoo until I'm 18 and it's legal.

'Elle doesn't need a tattoo, she's an Infinite through and through,' signs Kwesi. 'Now, time to eat!'

Guess what we're having to eat. Moi-moi, chin-chin and puff-puff as nibbles, served in little bowls. That's followed by all kinds of rice and vegan meat that tastes EXACTLY like the real thing. Vegan meat in 2050 IS the real thing. We don't sit at the table, we put it on paper plates, party style, and snuggle into bean bags. I find myself sitting near Ama and she lowers her voice.

'Elle, I've been thinking. Those cards from the Crystal Ball.'

'Yes, spooky,' I reply, remembering the cartoon grinning skeleton and the spider spinning a web; the unnerving feeling that someone was reading my mind. With all that's happened since, I'd forgotten about them.

'Your grandma died AND you trapped The Vicious Circle in your web of words,' says Ama. 'Maybe the machine didn't malfunction after all.'

'It was weird getting two cards. The place must be run by Leaplings who know all our business. Like Destiny.' I shudder. 'What about your black cat? Any luck?'

'Yeah, sis! Was waiting for the right moment to tell you. I got a date with MC^2!' She bites into her chickpea drumstick.

188

'That's brilliant, Ama! Where are you going?'

'A rhyme night in real time. He's doing a set but we get to hang out afterwards.' She pauses. 'It's a start.'

'I'm really pleased for you.'

Portia pulls up a bean bag. 'Want to hear my news?'

'You've been exited from The Vicious Circle?' guesses Ama. 'But it doesn't matter cos The Vicious Circle no longer exists.'

'No! Better than that. Destiny's been told to stop tampering with my Porsche. She never managed to tap into my phone. Millennia doesn't know I'm a double agent; I can still spy on her.'

'Hardly good news.' I can't help my bluntness. 'Destiny already knows about The Infinites. Remember the final note? Only a matter of time before she tells Millennia.' I pause. 'And right now, Millennia's desperate! I worry what she'll do next, now she's lost so many of her gang.'

'We'll soon find out,' replies Portia, changing her position on the bean bag. 'She and Destiny have been meeting a lot. I have to drive Millennia everywhere now The Grandfather's exited.'

'Guys, let's not talk about The Vicious Circle now,' says GMT. 'They're history; WE'RE the future! Let's have a toast to The Infinites. Robot, fill our glasses, please!'

Robot replenishes our home-made still lemonade and sparkling melon.

'To The Infinites,' we all say and clink glasses. 'ROOT FOR THE FUTURE!'

Chapter 00:00

A TIME TO BE BORN

'Grandma, when's your birthday?'

It's the 28th of December 2050. Big Ben and I have collected Grandma from the same date in 2002 to take her out on an adventure. We've luggaged her to 2050 so she can go on a bullet train. We're at Paddington Station, which looks so bright, shiny and high-tech compared to 1844, standing on the platform waiting for the 4.50 from Paddington to Penzance. I know she enjoys the rush of leaping through time and I want her to experience a different kind of rush, something between leaping and plane travel. Growing up, I never realised how much Grandma craves excitement. The last time I went back in time to visit her and offered to help clean the flat, she replied, blunt as ever:

'I am not Mrs Bleach and Grime; I did not marry my cleaning job. Sometimes I want adventure!'

Grandma wasn't at all surprised to see me and Big Ben, though it surprised me seeing a middle-aged version of her. It was true when she said before she died that she'd known me all her threescore and ten. I don't tell her Big Ben worked out she must therefore be 50 years old now and born in 1952, a leap year; or 51 if she was born between the 14th of November and the 28th of December 1951.

'What is my date of birth? Elle, have I not told you before? Why not ask this your enemy, Millennia, the same question?'

'Why do you say that, Grandma?' It's impossible to know how much Grandma knows from speaking with my future self.

'Visit year 2000 to find out.'

'Grandma, I don't care about Millennia, I care about you. If I knew your birthday, I could buy you a birthday present.'

Grandma smiles. 'I want Chronophone to plan your visits. So you don't appear like ghost and make me jump.'

'Brilliant, Grandma. I'll buy you a phone.'

'It must be the gold.'

'OK.'

'Train's arrived!' says Big Ben.

∞

We're sitting in our bubble in the First Class compartment. You can pay extra on mid-century bullet trains to have your own private space. People can see you and you can see them for safety but they can't hear your conversation. I love the adrenaline rush when the train accelerates out of the station. It's the closest I'll get to going on a fairground ride, speed but no weird spinning and none of the nausea! Big Ben loves it too; cars are still his specialist subject but fast trains come a close second.

Now we've caught the train and got settled, Big Ben opens a bag of corn crisps and I think about what Grandma just said.

'What does Millennia do in the year 2000? Can't you give me a clue, Grandma?'

Big Ben munches on a crisp. 'She was born on the 28th of February 1900.' He pauses. 'We were there.'

'What are you saying, BB?'

'The Grandfather said we had to go away unless we were a midwife.'

I remember the scene. The older version of The Grandfather trying to get rid of us because his daughter Rosalind was about to give birth; the teen version interrupting him.

'The Grandfather was about to become a grandfather,' I say, 'the moment Millennia was born.' I frown. 'But if Millennia was born on the 28th of February 1900—'

'Millennia's not a Leapling!' says Big Ben.

My mouth forms a capital O. I was so focused on the final note, I didn't clock the most important thing of all: Millennia's imminent birth.

'So that's why she's so obsessed with Leaplings. Imagine being born in an anti-leap year when your grandfather AND mother are both Leaplings with The Gift. She must have spent her whole life feeling inferior!'

'What if she was born the nanosecond between the 28th of February and the 1st of March?' says Big Ben, reminding me of the time we leapt at that moment from another anti-leap year, 2100. 'Then she might have a bit of Leap power.'

'Not likely,' I say. 'We were at the clockshop at 11 at night. It sounded like Rosalind was giving birth any minute.'

Grandma sucks her teeth. 'Millennia is an Annual but she won't accept it. She wants to be born in the leap year 2000. The millennium.'

'So that explains her name. Grandma, how do you know this? Are you Infinity?'

Grandma frowns. 'You ask too many question. One day, all will be revealed. Eat your sandwich!'

The train rushes through the countryside. I smile at Grandma being Grandma. I desperately want to know if she's Infinity but right now, it's important to enjoy each precious moment. I'm with my two favourite people in the world: Grandma and Big Ben. This is not a mission, it's a shopping trip, but it's still exciting. It's 2050 and Grandma will get her gold Chronophone. I bite into my sandwich. Plenty of time for missions in my future, even if they happen in the past. Plenty of time to conquer Millennia once and for all.

Acknowledgements

I live in a house of railfans. Most dinnertimes, trains of the past, present and future are centre stage in the conversation. So, having celebrated the 21st and 18th centuries in *The Infinite* and *The Time-Thief*, I couldn't resist setting some of *The Circle Breakers* in the 19th century, the Age of the Railway. I thank my boys, Solomon and Valentine, for converting me to trains and also my husband, Jeremy, for reading and commenting on an early draft and supporting me through hard times. Also, the brilliant and engaging book, *The Railways: Nation, Network and People* by Simon Bradley, proved invaluable for researching the Victorian era. As did the dated but absorbing *Samuel Coleridge-Taylor, Musician: His Life and Letters* by William Charles Berwick Sayers. I felt as if I'd met the maestro in person.

Thank you to the entire team at Canongate, for continuing to publish and celebrate The Leap Cycle series, especially my editor, Aa'Ishah Hawton, for your fantastic insights that helped me restructure an early draft and calibrate the tone. Katie

Huckstep, you did a fabulous job with the Zoom schools events and your technical support was an absolute godsend! Aisling Holling, I look forward to working with you on the tour. Alice Shortland, your continued support with my blog and Powerpoints is invaluable. Also, thank you Vicki Rutherford and Leila Cruikshank for accommodating my ever-changing deadlines in what proved to be a very challenging 2021. Your professionalism and compassion are much appreciated.

Thy Bui, the cover is amazing! Welcome to the Leap Cycle series. I look forward to seeing what you will come up with next.

A special thank you again, Lizzie Huxley-Jones, for another meticulous sensitivity read and your warm, enthusiastic response; your input is invaluable to this series.

Simon Trewin, you're a star! I hugely appreciate your upbeat outlook, wise words and our wonderful, occasional in-person meetings. Emily Hayward-Whitlock, thank you for your belief in the concept and all your hard work sending the books out into the world of film and TV. It was great to meet you on Zoom. Melanie Abrahams, Rochelle Saunders and the Renaissance One team, your behind-the-scenes support in the logistics of events is priceless.

So many of my friends and fellow writers, too many to name here, have sustained me in incalculable ways throughout this series. But a special thank you goes out to the following: Geoff Allnutt and Rosemary Harris for reading and commenting on an early draft; Steve Tasane for our decades-long literary debates that infinitely enlighten me as a writer and reader; Chris Bonnello for continuing the inspiring email exchange we began at the beginning of The Leap Cycle which has sustained me in my four-book journey and your own brilliant *Underdogs* series; Elle McNicoll, for your encouragement and for sharing with the world your line-up of superb neurodivergent heroines in a range of genres. How do you do it? Jasbinder Bilan for that magical, tropical Tŷ Newydd writing course; you were a joy to work with. And all my local friends who attended the event on LV21 last summer where I was finally able to launch the series in-person; it meant a lot that you were there.

Teachers, librarians, booksellers, bloggers, parents and arts promoters in the real and virtual worlds deserve a huge thank you for continuing to champion The Leap Cycle series. A special thank you to everyone at the Scottish Book Trust and BBC Scotland for inviting me onto Authors Live in Glasgow; Marianne Weekes, Librarian at Gravesend Grammar School, for inviting me to give a workshop-talk on science fiction to Year 7s and 8s on World Book Day 2022, and to Oliver Foulds for being my number one fan and the first teenager in the world to read *The Circle Breakers*; and Leusa Llewelyn, Director of Tŷ Newydd, National Writing Centre of Wales, and all the team for inviting me to teach a residential course: Books For All, writing for children and young adults. It was a brilliant opportunity to share my enthusiasm and insights over time.

Finally, as ever, thank you to the readers, young and old, 8 to ∞. I couldn't do this without you.